QUESTIONS FOR THE DEVIL

THE SENSITIVES BOOK FIVE

RICK WOOD

BLOOD SPLATTER PRESS

ABOUT THE AUTHOR

Rick Wood is a British writer born in Cheltenham.

His love for writing came at an early age, as did his battle with mental health. After defeating his demons, he grew up and became a stand-up comedian, then a drama and English teacher.

He now lives in Loughborough, where he divides his time between watching horror, reading horror, and writing horror.

ALSO BY RICK WOOD

The Sensitives:

Book One – The Sensitives

Book Two – My Exorcism Killed Me

Book Three – Close to Death

Book Four – Demon's Daughter

Book Five – Questions for the Devil

Book Six - Repent

Book Seven - The Resurgence

Book Eight - Until the End

Shutter House

Shutter House

Prequel Book One - This Book is Full of Bodies

Cia Rose:

Book One – After the Devil Has Won

Book Two – After the End Has Begun

Book Three - After the Living Have Lost

Chronicles of the Infected

Book One – Zombie Attack

Book Two – Zombie Defence

Book Three – Zombie World

Standalones:

When Liberty Dies

I Do Not Belong

Death of the Honeymoon

Sean Mallon:

Book One – The Art of Murder

Book Two – Redemption of the Hopeless

The Edward King Series:

Book One – I Have the Sight

Book Two – Descendant of Hell

Book Three – An Exorcist Possessed

Book Four – Blood of Hope

Book Five – The World Ends Tonight

Non-Fiction

How to Write an Awesome Novel

Thrillers published as Ed Grace:

The Jay Sullivan Thriller Series

Assassin Down

Kill Them Quickly

For Martin, who lived his life the way he wanted to live it.

This world would be better if we were all a little more like Uncle Martin.

Amalgamation (noun)

The action, process, or result of combining or uniting.

Incarnation (noun)

A person who embodies in the flesh a deity, spirit, or quality.

Amalgamation Incarnation (noun)

A person who has been under demonic possession for so long that the demon has taken that person's place on Earth, combining with that person's flesh to become the personified embodiment of that demon – permanently.

THEN

EVERY EXORCISM WAS THE SAME – IN THAT THEY WERE ALWAYS different to the last.

They always had screaming, objects flying, taunting, multiple voices through the same mouth. They all had tears, anger, relief, perseverance, and relentless testing of stamina. Each experience was a catastrophic insight that made you question everything you know about the world, everything you thought was real, and everything that could be meant by the words *God*, *Devil*, *Heaven*, and *Hell*.

The one thing that could undoubtedly be said about each exorcism was that it was undeniably, inarguably, conclusively, horrific.

This one was not like that.

This one was worse.

Father Connor O'Neil, in his limited experience, hadn't faced anything like this.

The demons plaguing their victims always showed off. Wind would encircle the exorcists, light objects would fly at them, and the bed would rattle.

This bed wasn't rattling. It was pounding in mid-air,

soaring to head height and staying there, shaking, tossing the poor child suffering through their torment back and forth. The child's screams could be heard amongst the demon's laughter, pleading with their incessant tormentor to cease their attack.

Light objects were flying around the exorcists, just like every other exorcism – but never had O'Neil seen a door fly from its hinges, and never had he been taken off his feet. His back pressed against the wall like he was nailed in place; his arms forcibly stretched wide as if he were on a crucifix, and it took him too long to believe that his immobility was actually real.

How was this happening?

A demon in the flesh of their victim doesn't have this kind of power on Earth. They have scare tactics, yes, and they can cause pain to those around them and agony to the person they inhabit – but they can't legitimately threaten a life in this way.

But this one could.

And it was loving every moment.

"From all sin, from your wrath, from sudden and provided death!" Father Elijah Harris, O'Neil's loyal and trusted mentor, persevered.

O'Neil attempted to pull his arms away, to take them off the wall, but the resistance was too much. He could feel fingers wrapped around his arms, muscles pushing him back; though there was nothing there, he could feel it.

"The response, O'Neil!" Harris demanded.

"Deliver us, oh Lord!" O'Neil responded, despite the broken pieces of chair battering against his stationary body, despite his constant struggling against his grave predicament.

"From the snares of the devil, from anger, hatred, and ill will!"

"Deliver us, oh–"

Something clamped around his throat. Something tight, something that could not be seen but could be felt, even smelt, its potent pang of repulsive musk. Thick, wiry claws tucked around his gullet, squeezing as he choked, choking on his words and finding that he could not speak.

Even worse, he found that he could not breathe.

"Father..." he tried, his voice coming out in a croak. "Harris..."

Harris looked over his shoulder and bestowed his fateful eyes upon his apprentice. Pinned to the wall, suffocating, losing his ability to live.

Harris poised on this image for seconds, though they felt like hours. His eyes hovered over the desperate countenance of a man distraught, a man fearing inevitable death.

Harris turned back to the child, the bed shaking the young victim in a salvo of attacks.

This wasn't right.

A demon couldn't do this.

They couldn't.

That is, unless...

Harris made a decision.

"Lord, forgive me for what I am about to do," Harris spoke, disregarding the rites of exorcism, his crucifix slipping from his sweaty fingers and landing in a clang upon the splintered wooden floorboards.

"Harris..." O'Neil continued to suffer, continued to plead though his voice was lost.

Harris took a step toward the battering bed.

"I know my words can't save me, my prayer can't save me, only Christ can save me," Harris persisted, placing his hands on the end of the bed, waiting until he had a good enough grip to hoist himself up, climb over the edge and dangle, doing all he could to keep his grip.

O'Neil felt the room slip away. Felt his thoughts descend to the nonsensical utterances of sparse words. It felt like falling asleep, except harder.

"By faith I gratefully receive your gift of salvation, should you choose to bestow it upon me."

Harris slid himself up, onto the bed, keeping both arms and both legs firmly on the wiry indents of the mattress, balancing, doing all he could to keep steady.

The face of the child was marked with a pale staleness that would not be ridded. Its childish features had faded away, turning a soft smile to a cocky leer.

From his inside pocket, Harris withdrew a knife. A sharp, pointed, steel knife.

"Thank you, Lord, Jesus, for coming to Earth, dying for our sins and rising, for you give the gift of eternal life."

He raised his knife high above his head.

"Come into my heart, Lord Jesus, and be my saviour."

He plunged the knife downwards, into the child's chest.

"Amen."

He lifted the knife up and plunged it downwards again.

Again. Again. Again.

Then, with a final stroke of its blade, he ran its sharp entrapment across the coarse skin of the child's throat.

The bed collapsed to the ground.

The objects circling the air collapsed to the ground.

O'Neil collapsed to the ground.

His breath heaved, quick, desperate, in, out, in, out, in out in out in out.

He relished the oxygen. Was grateful for the air. Thankful in a way he'd never been.

He dropped onto his back.

His mind returned. His thoughts reformed. His body responded to him once again.

That was when he realised what Father Elijah Harris had just done.

"Father?" O'Neil said, pushing himself up into a seated position. "Father, what have you done?"

Harris didn't respond. His head remained bowed, his resolve fading, his cheeks damp.

"Father?" O'Neil said once again, reality registering, horrifying him. He leapt to his feet, stumbled under the dizziness of his concussion, and threw himself to the side of the bed.

Harris didn't move. He sat, head bowed, eyes gone.

O'Neil looked over the body. Numerous wounds upon the chest, gaping open, holes granting insight to the inner realms of the victim's body. Its throat, a steady slice across, blood still dribbling over the red-drenched bed sheets.

"Father?" O'Neil repeated. "Why did you do this? This is not what we do, why did you do this?"

His mentor shook his head.

"Father?" O'Neil said again.

"Oh, shut it, would you!" Harris barked. "To hell with you!"

"But you–"

"You're young, you know nothing of this world. Shut up until you have listened."

"Okay, Father. I'm listening."

Harris went to speak, but didn't. He was prepared to explain to his young follower who needed answers, then he wasn't; the words would not form.

"It was too late," Harris sobbed. "*We* were too late."

"But I thought an exorcism would–"

"Did you not hear me tell you to shut up?"

O'Neil fell silent.

"Sometimes…" Harris said, shaking his head, finding his words. "Sometimes there is nothing we can do, when the demon has been there for so long."

"So you killed the child?"

"I didn't kill the child," Harris said. "The child had been gone for a long time. There was no child left."

A FEW WEEKS AGO

2

Oscar's fingertips placed themselves upon April's. He held them there, the light grace of her skin caressing his, like magic, like love – he could feel it, that love; he could feel it from deep inside of him, bursting through his weakening muscles to those fingertips that pressed so delicately against hers.

She looked back at him, almost like a mirror. Their facial expressions echoing each other, smiles, fluttering eyes, shaking breaths.

"April," Oscar said, then stopped. He didn't know what he was going to say. He knew what he wanted to say; well, he had the gist of it. The words he wanted to verbalise weren't coming out.

She said nothing. Just looked back at him. Silent. Sweet.

"April, I–" he tried again.

His voice fought against his thoughts.

"April, I – I'm sorry."

He didn't look up at her.

He couldn't.

But he must.

So he did.

She didn't look back.

She withdrew her fingertips.

"April, what's–"

"My chest, it hurts," she said, so blankly, so cold.

"I know, I feel it too."

"No, Oscar, my chest – it hurts."

He looked down. Her hands rested over her heart and, between her fingers, blood trickled. She lifted her face to his as if he had a solution, as if there was something she could do. Despair wiped across her eyes, her diluted-red cheeks, her perspiring forehead. Every piece of her reached out to him, willing him to do something.

He reached out his hands and placed them on her arms.

"April, it'll be okay," he lied.

She shook her head. Pulled herself away from his grip.

"Oscar," she said again. "My chest…"

"April–"

"My chest…"

"April, we can–"

"My chest!"

His eyes opened.

He turned to see if April was okay.

She wasn't there. It was another dream. He was alone. On the dank floor of a shop window in Rome. Already, the sun was giving the sky a gentle illumination, a warm breeze was bustling past him, and tourists were ignoring him like he was dirt.

He stood, opening his bag, checking nothing had been stolen during the night. He still had what little he had left. Enough money for his next trip, wherever that would be. Nothing more.

The Vatican had told him to stay away. That they couldn't speak there. Oscar had insisted. And this was the compromise.

A few miles away, on the edge of Vatican City. As close as

they would let him. Mopeds sped by. Pollution fought the air. You couldn't walk down a street without seeing another broken-down block of flats.

He checked the road sign. Via Alberto Cadlolo.

It was the right place, it was dawn, but no one was there.

Then again, why would they show up?

No, Oscar was confident. They didn't want him in the centre of their city, making a fuss, disgracing the Church – revealing that exorcism was alive and well in today's world, and what's more, it was being performed by a non-priest. Something called a Sensitive.

But then again, what is a Sensitive, really?

Oscar shook his head. If he knew the answer, he wouldn't be there.

Memories of his dream grew on him as his mind adjusted to being awake.

God, he missed April.

It had been a matter of weeks, and already he was longing for her. Aching to be back beside her.

He wondered if she'd even wait for him. How long until she stopped bothering? Moved on?

He could just picture Julian next to her: "He's a loser, you can do better, he abandoned you."

Of course, it wasn't as simple as that. She'd given birth to what turned out to be a demon in child's clothing. Oscar was oblivious to everything – the child grew to be a toddler within months, but its ability to mask his perception was all too skilful. In the end, Oscar had nearly killed April defending that demon.

April, his dream; the woman he'd die for that he almost killed.

It wasn't fair.

Most of all, it wasn't right.

He was a Sensitive. A conception of Heaven. Surely, with

his *gift* – as it was always referred to – he'd be able to resist such things, or at least have an awareness. The way its hypnotic hold exerted so much control over him was scary. He was better than that.

And he needed to find out more.

What he was. What it meant. Why Sensitives even existed, and what their purpose was in this world.

His dream, however, was not a dream about abandonment. It was about death. Maybe that's what he was most scared of – what would happen without him there to protect her.

Then again, what would happen without her to protect him?

And could he be sure it wasn't himself he was protecting her from?

Across the street, a man made a brief eye contact with Oscar. Beneath a large coat, Oscar saw the priest's collar. This was him. This was the sign.

He made his way over.

"I was wondering whether you were going to show," Oscar said.

"With the fuss you made?" the priest retorted, not bothering to disguise his judgemental sneer. "We were obligated to keep you away."

Rude, really. Oscar had fought their war for years. Had lost friends to their war. Had done it all in their name – and this was how they repaid him?

"Let's keep this quick then," Oscar decided. "What have you got for me?"

The priest handed Oscar an envelope.

"He lives in Edinburgh," the priest stated.

"I thought he was Irish?"

"He is, he just lives in Edinburgh."

"Why?"

The priest narrowed his eyes and shook his head at Oscar

like he was a vagabond begging for change. "How the heck would I know?"

Well, this is a lovely, warm reception, isn't it! Oscar thought. Then again, was he expecting anything else after his previous confrontation?

"Does he know I'm coming?"

"Yes. But do not expect a warm welcome. He's not particularly partial to company."

"Fine," he said, trying not to bite. "Looks like I have what I need. Seems like we can part ways."

"Thank goodness," the priest spitefully spat, then left, pulling his coat around himself and checking the street for any onlookers.

Oscar opened the envelope. Inside was a piece of paper with the address of Father Connor O'Neil.

He hailed a taxi.

"Aeroporto, per favour," he requested, saying goodbye to Italy as they left.

NOW

3

EDINBURGH WAS A BEAUTIFUL CITY.

Oscar had grown up in a small town called Tewkesbury, in Gloucestershire – it wasn't the most hustling and bustling of places. The most commotion you'd get would be when a pensioner fell over or a dog walker lost control of their lead. As a result, Oscar hadn't become particularly accustomed to the fevered hive of cities, and found them slightly intimidating.

Edinburgh was the exception.

It was still a city, sure enough – but it had an air of grace about it. It had still managed to retain its rustic, old-fashioned buildings without having to give way to an overload of modern complexes – although there were a few, but mainly in the centre of town. When he had arrived, he'd made his way off Edinburgh Waverley train station and looked upon a city full of life, but without the nervous apprehension he'd feel with over-crowded places. The city was open, which made the mass of people seem more spread out, and he decided straight away that this would be a perfect place to live.

He walked the few miles out of the town centre, following his map to Royal Circus Lane. There, he found a single-track brick road between a set of houses. Normally a side street down a single-track road would make you worry about the lack of life and light, wondering who may be lurking, but this was not so; the houses were quaint, with light-brown bricks of various sizes giving them a gentle feel, like no one bad could possibly dwell in them. Hedges were deliberately positioned up some of the walls, often deliberately forming an arch over doorways in a way that may welcome someone important home.

So this was where Oscar would find him.

Father Connor O'Neil.

He withdrew the paper he'd taken from Derek's journal and unfolded it, feeling slightly ashamed for the wrinkled nature of the paper's state – Derek would be cross to see his prize works in such condition. Oscar read it once more.

Father Connor O'Neil, an Irish priest, was the first to feel something changing. I knew about the coming of the Sensitives from an angel's message, but O'Neil felt it in his bones. To him, something altered, something shifted, and he recognised it.

I should probably give O'Neil some backstory at this point. He was a decorated exorcist. Not decorated in the literal sense, of course; an exorcist always works in the shadows of the Church – but he had received multiple congratulations from the Church for his services in ridding the world of demonic possession. He'd worked under Father Elijah Harris, another experienced exorcist, but one who was old-fashioned. Father Harris had begun his career during the Second World War. Events of such evil always require demonic intervention. Humans aren't capable of such evil without a push, which meant that Harris began his career when possession was rife, and common, and frequent – he grew up in a world that was plagued in a way we couldn't know. Where I fought a demon every month or so, he would be fighting two to three a week.

As such, he made quite an impression on O'Neil. I first met him in the late nineties, when O'Neil was in his late twenties. He was young and impressionable, slightly naïve, but extraordinarily gifted.

People do not come without their flaws, however.

O'Neil was not the same man when I met him again, in the aftermath of the Edward King war. There was something different about him. There were no smiles, no handshakes – just a very cold, bitter man.

He told me he could feel a rumble in the heavens. That he knew something was coming. I told him about the Sensitives, and his eyes lit up in recognition.

I asked him what the Sensitives could do, what they could mean.

He didn't answer.

He refused an answer.

And he refused to talk to me again.

Oscar sighed.

Was he expecting a warm welcome?

Hell, he had no idea what to expect. He had experienced all kinds of people in this fight, from all walks of life, but rarely had he experienced someone who was glad to be in the world of demon-fighting.

Standing before a dainty house on the curve of the street, the only one cast entirely in shadow, he took a deep breath in.

He placed four clear knocks on the front door.

4

An Irish coffee, and the morning had begun.

Shame about having to spoil the Irish coffee with coffee.

O'Neil leant back in his chair, the wooden arm rests splintering his elbow and broken springs denting his numb leg. He'd only been out of bed for an hour and already he was bemoaning the onset of morning. Another pointless day for him to sit around, getting restless, talking to no one.

Maybe he should get a dog.

Then again, that would imply he could give enough of a shit about something to feed it and clean it and walk it, and he felt far more comfortable as a recluse, sitting silently in his own feeble contemplation, ruing the world and the grief it brought with it. In all honesty, if he had a dog, he'd probably kill it.

He almost fell back to sleep until he was woken by four clear knocks on the front door.

"Argh," he snarled. "For feck sake."

What if he just left them?

What was it, the postman?

Who would be sending him post?

Either way, there would be nothing worth getting out of his seat for.

He relaxed back into his chair. It was an old chair with not much comfort left in it, but he had a bond with that chair, and he wasn't about to trade it in; that would mean having to walk around shops with people talking and laughing and living, and it was much better just sitting there, feeling the wiry indents press sharply against his lower back.

Four clear knocks again.

"Jesus," he muttered.

He stood. Caught a glimpse of himself in the mirror. His greyed hair, short and spiked, stood on end, having been left unwashed and stuck to a pillow for twelve hours at a time – and his priest's collar poked guiltily from beneath his throat.

He scoffed every time he saw it. But he had to wear it. It was all about appearances. Besides, getting changed wasn't worth the effort.

He trudged down the stairs, knocking into the bare walls as he did.

The knocks again.

"A'right, a'right, I'm coming!" he growled.

He reached the door. Went to open it, found it locked.

How do you unlock it again?

He took off the chain. Went to open it.

Locked.

He stood back. Surveyed the door. It couldn't be that hard. This was why he never bothered opening it.

Finally, he found it. A lock he needed to turn beneath the handle. He twisted it and opened the door.

There stood a young man, mid-twenties, skinny, messy. Not too tidy and put together, but far more than O'Neil was.

"What?" he barked.

"Hi," the fellow introduced himself, "I'm Oscar. The Church told me you were expecting me."

The Church?

What?

Oh, yes. That phone call that had woken him up yesterday.

They had said to expect someone.

Could he really be bothered?

"I was wondering if I could talk to–"

O'Neil slammed the door in Oscar's face.

He went to stumble back into his dark and dank house. He had a busy afternoon of wallowing in self-pity and he wasn't prepared to interrupt it.

He stopped.

Then again, this kid had come to see him. He'd been warned.

Four knocks resounded once more.

Four, always four, why four? Couldn't the irritating ball of youthful joy shake it up somehow?

He turned and marched back to the door, swinging it open, causing it to creak against its unused hinges.

"What?" he barked again.

"I, er…" Oscar stumbled. "I'm sorry, did I offend you?"

"No, no," O'Neil replied, rubbing his head, flinching at the distant sun in the open sky. "Fine, it's fine. What do you want?"

"Well, I was hoping I might be able to talk to you."

O'Neil stood and waited.

"Fine. Talk."

Oscar opened his mouth to find no words. O'Neil could see his face trying to make sense of the situation, of what to do. O'Neil almost felt sorry for the lad – *almost.* Clearly, the boy had not met the world yet.

Maybe it was O'Neil's job to make the introduction.

"Fine, fine," O'Neil said, waving away some imaginary discomfort from the air. "Come in."

O'Neil opened the door and allowed Oscar in, unintentionally slamming the door behind him.

"Living room is this way," O'Neil said, leading Oscar through. He could feel Oscar's judgement; the curtains were drawn, the sofas were the shade of brown your grandparents would probably have in their living room, and the floor was covered in various plates and cups and pieces of food O'Neil had discarded and forgotten about.

"I suppose I should offer you a coffee," O'Neil said.

"If you wouldn't mind," Oscar responded. So polite, so well-mannered. O'Neil didn't know whether to envy it or pity it.

O'Neil made his way into the kitchen, which was just as unkempt. He made a weak coffee with milk two days past its expiry date and shoved it in Oscar's face.

"Thank you," Oscar responded, sitting on the edge of the sofa and tenderly holding his cup.

"So what do you–"

O'Neil stopped.

He looked upon the boy.

The boy was a Sensitive.

He could feel it.

This was him.

This was what he was waiting for.

The reason he had bothered to stay.

His purpose for hanging around in this shitty little life.

"Ah," O'Neil said, then disguised his astonishment. "So, what have you come here for?"

"Answers."

"Answers?" O'Neil responded with a mocking laugh. "Pah! I bet you barely even know the questions!"

He stared some more. Marvelled. Rubbed his hands together.

A Sensitive.

Yes, he finally had purpose. He finally had a reason to put up with the world.

He had waited here for so long. Knowing that this would come. Knowing that this was his purpose.

Salvation had arrived.

5

Oscar wasn't sure what to make of Father O'Neil. In all honesty, most exorcists he'd met who were more toward the end of their careers weren't always the epitome of good mental health, but something just seemed oddly peculiar about him.

There was an absence about his face, yet a presence about his eyes. He was permanently pale, yet his irises had the most intense colour he could see, despite them having no constant colour; they were easy changeable between blue, green, and brown from one minute to the next, and it reminded him of a friend he'd had at primary school whose eyes did the same.

As O'Neil led Oscar up the stairs that sank and moaned with every step, Oscar noted a strange slant in the way O'Neil walked. It wasn't so much a limp, but a hunch to the side that rose and deflated with every movement.

O'Neil opened the door to a bedroom.

"This is where you can stay," he said. "I'm not promising it'll be much of a craic, but it'll keep you dry from the rain."

"What else can you hope for from a room?" Oscar joked, but O'Neil's face held onto its grimace like it was carved in stone.

"Let me know if you need anything," O'Neil said disingenuously, and went to leave.

"Wait," Oscar said, prompting O'Neil to pause. "When – when can I ask you my questions?"

"Questions?" O'Neil frowned. "You don't."

"But that's why I'm here."

"I'm not interested in any questions. Don't ask any, and I won't have to tell you I haven't the foggiest."

"Then what can you tell me?"

O'Neil snorted.

"I can tell you nuttin'. But I can show you what I can, that's the best I can offer you."

"I guess that will have to do."

"You guess?" O'Neil shook his head. "You better be a bit more bleedin' grateful than that!"

"What now?" Oscar asked. "What do we do now?"

O'Neil grimaced.

"Nothin'. We do nothin'. We start tomorrow."

"Well, what am I supposed to do until then?"

"What does that concern me?"

O'Neil looked at Oscar like he'd just asked him what two plus two is. He slammed the door, and Oscar could hear the steps growing faint as he plodded across the corridor.

Oscar looked around himself. There were prison cells bigger than this room. What's more, half of the ceiling was sloped, meaning he could only stand up fully in one half. A single bed with a plain, grey bedsheet just about fit the length of the room, and there was a broken wicker chair in the corner.

He dumped his bag and lay on the bed, staring at the ceiling, which was closer to his face than he was used to.

He sighed.

So this was the great exorcist who had the answers. The man Derek had written about, citing that O'Neil could explain what it was to be a Sensitive, could explain how he'd felt the coming of multiple gifts from Heaven.

He looked like Hell dragged backwards through a hedge.

Oscar opened his bag and reached in, not needing to look, knowing where in his bag the item he was searching for was situated. He withdrew the envelope and opened it, placing the photographs it held on his lap, lifting them to his eyes one by one.

He and April on a summer's day having a picnic.

April smiling at him as he took a selfie of them their first morning living together.

He and April with... their daughter. Hayley.

No, not their daughter.

April in a wheelchair.

How did that one get in?

He ripped it in half, crumpled it into a ball, and threw it to the floor. He'd pick it up later.

Then he found his favourite photo. Her purple hair flowing across her shoulders, her nose stud shining in the glimmer of the sun, her smile making him melt all over again.

Wow, I miss her.

It wasn't just a little fleeting thought or feeling of absence – it was a wrenching pain in the pit of his gut. A deep yearning that quelled his appetite. A constant aching of his chest, tension in his mind, pulling on his thoughts.

She was always there. Always behind everything.

He wished he could see her. Touch her.

Just talk to her.

But he couldn't.

He'd tried to kill her. Under the influence of a demon, yes, but that demon had been powerful enough to turn him into–

No.

He needed to stop this.

Deliberating wouldn't change what happened.

Overthinking wouldn't solve his guilt. Wouldn't make the pain go away.

He put the photographs back in the envelope and put the envelope back into the bag. He pushed the envelope to the bottom of the bag, just as he pushed the thoughts to the back of his mind.

He closed his eyes and hoped that, tonight, he wouldn't have to dream about her.

THEN

6

T$_{\text{HE}}$ S$_{\text{EAT}}$ A$_{\text{T}}$ T$_{\text{HE}}$ B$_{\text{ACK}}$ O$_{\text{F}}$ T$_{\text{HE}}$ A$_{\text{UDITORIUM}}$ A$_{\text{LWAYS}}$ H$_{\text{AD}}$ T$_{\text{HE}}$ worst view, but O'Neil had little choice.

Besides, there wasn't a chance he was going to miss this.

It was barely even an auditorium anyway. It was a school hall. It was hardly like being stuck at the back of an arena, wondering if the people on stage were even the people you'd paid to see or whether they were lookalikes conning you out of your money. He could see the play clearly as it was.

And this was the way that Aubrey's mother wanted it. O'Neil out of sight.

As for the Church – well, they'd have a meltdown if they knew he was within a mile of Aubrey. A priest breaking his celibacy, for however fleeting temptation it was, was bad enough; to have a daughter out of it was even worse. He was lucky they hadn't expelled him.

The cynic in him would argue that every priest he knew broke their vow all the time, whereas his indiscretion occurred once. Then again, unlike other priests, his indiscretion had created permanent evidence of his sin in the form of his daughter.

Watching her on stage, star of the school play, like a tiny person playing at being big, he was willing to give it all up. The call of the exorcist could wait. He was beaming with pride, and he wanted to scream from the top of the building that she was his. He wanted to parade her down the streets, showering her with praise, telling anyone he met that this was his beautiful girl and he didn't care who knew it.

Natasha turned and saw him. She was sat a few rows back from the front with her husband and, from the look on her face, he could tell he was the last person she'd wanted to see. Her scowl told him exactly what she was thinking, and he wasn't sure what he was more scared of – the devil, or her.

The play ended, and the parents graciously applauded. Aubrey's teacher led them all out to the front and coerced them into taking a bow. He didn't envy the job she had, cajoling a group of toddlers into a prolonged, coordinated concentrated activity – but she'd done brilliantly.

And there she was, his daughter, centre stage.

Natasha turned to her husband – O'Neil didn't know his name – and told him she was going to the toilet. With an elated wave at Aubrey, she marched to the back of the school hall and jabbed her finger at O'Neil.

"Outside," she demanded. "Now."

She charged outside and waited in the corridor, leaning all her weight on one leg, biting her nails, huffing loud enough for him to hear.

O'Neil finished applauding and reluctantly followed her out.

"What the hell are you doing here?" she scolded, before he'd even fully emerged from the hall.

"Nat–" O'Neil put his hand out in an attempt to calm her. If anything, it just woke the beast inside.

"Do not Nat me," she responded. "Answer the question – what the hell are you doing here?"

"I'm here to see my daughter in her play."

"See your daughter? She's not your daughter! She is my husband's daughter!"

"No, she's not."

"As far as the world's concerned she is."

"I don't need them to know. I only need Aubrey to–"

"Well, she doesn't."

"Then I'll tell her."

"Ooh, you dare, I will have that collar taken off or tightened until you choke."

"The Church knows, Nat."

"Stop calling me Nat!"

O'Neil sighed. Gathered his thoughts. Placed his arm on the wall, covered in amateurish paintings of plants and families.

"You can't stop me from seeing her," he said, his voice soft and calm.

"You idiot! How do you think this makes you look? As far as everyone in there is concerned, you're just some weirdo priest come to watch over all the little kiddies and applaud as they dance and do their play. You look like a freak."

"Is this about me being a priest?"

"No, it's not, it's not about that, it's about–" she stopped herself. Wiped the sweat from her brow. She was shaking.

"Say it," O'Neil said.

"Shut up."

"No, go on, say it. It's about me being…"

"You know what you do."

"An exorcist."

She rolled her eyes.

"I know you don't believe in all that," O'Neil said, which prompted a folding of the arms. "But that shouldn't have anything to do with it."

"Believe in it or not, what you do is dangerous."

"Ah, so that's the real reason."

"Yes! Yes, it is! Can you really guarantee, in your heart of hearts, in your pathetic priest oath – however useless that would be – that she would be safe? With you as her father, that she'd never be in danger?"

O'Neil paused. How could he answer that? He couldn't be dishonest.

"Are we ever not in danger, in a world like this?" O'Neil tried.

"What a ridiculous argument!"

"Nat, I've done what you've asked. I've said nothing to your husband, I've allowed this charade to go on, I've seen her in the capacity you'd allow – as her priest, as a spiritual mentor. Are you really saying now that–"

"I don't want you to see her. Yes, that's what I'm saying."

O'Neil didn't know what to say. He lifted his hands in the air and looked for the words, but they were not forthcoming.

"Well… that's not fair," he came out with.

"Not fair? You want to talk to me about not fair? How about falling for a priest who's more in love with some God who couldn't care less than–"

She stopped herself. Wiped her eyes.

"You know you can't keep me away. When she's old enough, I'll tell her. She'll know the truth."

"When she's old enough, she'll know well enough not to care."

With those final words hanging in the air like a potent stench, she marched back into the school hall, where she was reunited with Aubrey. She hoisted her up in her arms, her demeanour changing in an instant, and kissed her daughter repeatedly on the cheeks, repeating over and over how proud she was, how wonderful Aubrey had been in the play.

Her husband nodded at O'Neil, oblivious.

O'Neil watched his daughter hug the man who thought he was her dad.

O'Neil turned and left.

He had wars to wage and battles to fight.

This was just one of them – and it wasn't over.

NOW

7

OSCAR ROSE FROM THE ASHES, THE GROUND BENEATH HIM decorated with the images of a thousand corpses, all burnt to a crisp.

He floated mid-air, holding his hands out, feeling power surge through him like a bullet slowly coursing through his body, destroying his insides then bringing them back to life again, but stronger.

He screamed, and his roar came out in a rumble that shook the Earth.

Beneath him was Derek. Martin. O'Neil. All looking up at him, looking to him with beseeching eyes, begging him to stop.

Julian attacked him, but with a quick swipe of his hand, Julian's throat was gushing with seas of red, wave after wave, rushing between the cracks of the dead, filling the ground Oscar rose above like a pool.

Then there was April.

On her knees, looking up to him, her arms out.

"Please," she begged.

"I love you," she begged.

"Just stop this," she begged.

Oscar just laughed.

Shook his head piteously.

She cried.

He felt nothing. No sympathy, no pain, no reaction to watching her crumble. He was empty, full up with freedom, liberated from the weak and feeble mind of a human. He no longer suffered from overthinking, from procrastination, from worrying about where his aimless life was wandering.

This was the end of it.

This was the end of everything.

"My chest!" she cried, clutching her heart. "My chest hurts."

He lifted his arm out. April rose, hanging by a non-existent noose, feet dangling, her arms still reaching out for him.

"My chest..."

He laughed.

"This is what they sent?" he asked, but it wasn't his voice. It was big, deep, booming, like it was being playing through a loud stereo system.

"Oscar," she begged.

"Don't," she begged.

"I–"

He stuck his hand into her chest and clutched her thudding heart in his claw. He looked her in the eyes as he squeezed it, harder, squeezing until he felt it bursting against his fingers, pressing against the prison of his hand, firing its juices against the containment of her ribs, drenching his hand in glory.

Her limp body fell to the floor, landing atop a multitude of skulls.

And he was happy.

His own screaming woke him up.

"Wake up!" said a voice with a strong Irish accent.

His mind struggled to comprehend, stuck between dreaming and awake.

"Wake up, for feck sake!"

He turned his head. Readjusted. Where was he? Who was this haggard, grey-haired priest above him?

"Wake up, you ponce! Wake up, or I'll beat the morning into you!"

For a moment, he thought he was being attacked.

Then he remembered. Father Connor O'Neil. The tiny room in Edinburgh. The grumpy bastard who'd given him accommodation.

"Okay, okay," Oscar objected. "I'm awake."

"Stop olagonin' and get yourself up, there's a coffee waiting for you."

"I'll be right down."

O'Neil stumbled out of the room, crouched as if he was used to the sloping ceiling, and Oscar listened to the steps pounding the weak floorboards as they descended down the stairs.

He sat up, placing his legs over the side of the bed, rubbing his face.

He looked to his watch. It was seven in the morning. He'd been asleep for almost sixteen hours.

"Jesus," he muttered to himself.

He stood and meandered through to the bathroom. It was barely big enough for him to fit in. The shower looked unused and complicated – a number of things for him to turn in order to get it working. The lavatory had a large chain and a big back. Everything was a sickly beige colour. It was as if the room hadn't been updated since the 1980s.

He went to the toilet, then stood over the sink. He splashed water on his face and looked himself in the mirror. He looked a mess. But, compared to O'Neil, he looked like the winner of a beauty contest. He was sure it wouldn't be noticed.

Then, as if the sight of his own eyes prompted some magical resurgence of his subconscious, his dream re-manifested itself.

He saw April's dying face once more.

Was this an omen?

Some kind of vision?

Was April in danger?

More than likely, this was probably his sub-conscious bullying him. Showing him sights he knew would kill him.

That familiar pang struck him in the gut. That absence he carried around without her.

What he'd give to talk to her.

But he couldn't.

Not yet.

"Hurry up, lad!"

He was being beckoned.

He dried his face and walked downstairs.

8

By the time Oscar had arrived in the kitchen there was a weak cup of instant coffee waiting for him, next to a slice of burnt toast coated in layers of butter.

At least there was some element of hospitality, he decided. From the impression of O'Neil Oscar had made the previous night, voluntarily being given breakfast seemed like a rare commodity, and he needed to make the most of it.

"Right you are, lad," O'Neil greeted Oscar, holding a coffee that was half drunk. An open bottle of whiskey beside the sink gave Oscar a good idea of what the coffee's main ingredient was. "C'mon then, once you foddered, we'll find out what I can do for you."

"Once I've what?"

From O'Neil's expectant stare, Oscar concluded that meant eating. O'Neil watched him intently, as if he'd just cooked a marvellous Sunday roast and was awaiting a verdict from a renowned food critic.

Oscar slowly realised this meant he was going to have to eat it.

He picked up the piece of toast, feeling the grease of the

butter run down his fingers, and placed it in his mouth, feeling numerous juices squelch onto his tongue as his teeth bit down.

"Mm," he said as he placed the toast back down.

Oscar and O'Neil made their way to the living room, in the process of which, Oscar's breakfast conveniently disappeared. Once Oscar had sat down, he noticed that the curtains were still closed and, despite it being a beautiful day outside, there was little to no light. In fact, the features of O'Neil's face were covered in shade, and he had to look carefully to be able to make out the minute subtleties of O'Neil's facial expressions. So far, Oscar had only seen two – perturbed and irritable.

"Do you mind if I open a curtain?" Oscar asked.

"Yes," O'Neil replied.

Oscar waited, as if there was going to be some explanation, some further elaboration of why the curtains needed to remain closed. But it was not forthcoming. O'Neil just sat there, watching Oscar, his hands clasped together.

"It's just, it's such a sunny day outside."

"No, it isn't," O'Neil argued.

Oscar briefly wondered whether he had actually seen the sun – but no, between the narrow crack of the blackout curtains, a vague burst of life tried to creep in.

"There is no such thing as a sunny day," O'Neil said. "It's all a lie. Sunny days don't come to people like us, and we don't deserve them."

Oscar wondered whether O'Neil had intended for those words to sound wise – because they didn't. They just sounded like ramblings of a drunk who had little idea why they were drunk in the first place.

"In Derek's journal," Oscar said, deciding to leave the subject, "it said that when the Sensitives came about, following the Edward King war" – O'Neil flinched at the name of Edward King – "you felt it. Whilst most were aware of it, you actually felt something change."

"Yes," O'Neil reluctantly concurred. "I guess I did say something to that effect."

"What is it you felt?"

O'Neil looked down at his hands for what seemed like an age. If it weren't for the croaking breaths of O'Neil's worn throat, Oscar might have been inclined to think that the man had abruptly fallen dead.

"I felt a bunch of fools rise," he finally answered. "I felt ability mixed with stupidity."

"You think Sensitives are stupid?"

"No." He thought. "And yes."

"I – I don't understand."

"I think that a man who doesn't have the abilities you have could still do a good job. I managed."

"But aren't Sensitives supposed to have been conceived by Heaven?"

O'Neil scoffed.

"Heaven? Pah!" He shook his head. "You think being a Sensitive means you have the ability? Yes. But the experience?"

"Surely experience comes with the path we are forced on. I've defeated enough to demons to–"

"Defeated!" O'Neil repeated, followed by an overzealous guffaw. "You never defeated anything."

"I assure you, I–"

"You talk about acquired experience, experience that comes with battles. My lad, you are facing an ancient evil who's been wreaking havoc and fighting fools like you and me for thousands of years – and you wonder why, when you try and exorcise them, they laugh at you?"

"Then what's the point?"

"The point? There is no point. You think a successful exorcism is a victory? No, you're just causing enough fuss that they'll leave and find an easier victim. All you can do is spend your life delaying the inevitable."

Oscar said nothing.

What was there to say to that?

He twisted his head and looked to an absent spot on the floor, leaving his mind to wonder whether this man's cynicism was accurate, or just that – cynicism.

"Then why bother?" Oscar said, though he knew he didn't mean it.

"Why bother? For your own fate, if no one else's."

"This is supposed to be a selfless path."

"Selfless? Here, I want to show you something. Put your shoes on."

O'Neil stood and fetched his coat – despite it being sweaty-hot weather outside.

Oscar put his shoes on then stood by the fireplace, at which time he noticed something. A little bell. Red and dainty.

Curiosity caught him and, though he wasn't sure why, he picked it up and rang it.

"Stop!" barked O'Neil.

Oscar immediately put the bell down.

"Do not ring that bell!" O'Neil demanded.

"Why not?"

"Because that is the bell I used through the years, before it was me alone here – it was a warning. Should one of us be in trouble, we ring the bell and warn the other exorcists. Until you picked it up, it hadn't been rung in years."

"Then what's the harm in me ringing it?"

"Just don't."

Oscar looked back at the bell. Was O'Neil paranoid? War-wounded? Or, as was quite likely – just insane?

"Come on," O'Neil said, and left the house.

Oscar took a big, deep breath inwards, wondering what he was about to be shown, and followed O'Neil into the street.

9

"MIND YOUR STEP," O'NEIL SAID. "AND MIND YOUR NOODLE."

Oscar followed O'Neil down a large set of descending stone steps. They seemed to be leading to nowhere. Despite the sun beaming overhead, they were now encased in darkness, a moisture hanging on the air and damp on the steps. It was as if the lower these steps went, the more detached they became from the outside world.

"Er, O'Neil," Oscar said, lifting his arms out to steady himself – if he wasn't going to slip on the wetness of the steps, it was going to be the uneven surface with sporadically placed bumps. "Where exactly are we going?"

"Oh, you'll see, my lad," O'Neil said, parading forward like the texture of the surface had no impact on him. Eventually, he led Oscar to a brick road, hidden beneath bridges. A chill crossed the air, hugging Oscar in its cold arms. When he stepped out the door that morning, he never would have thought he'd regret not bringing a jacket.

"Where are we?" Oscar asked, but his question went unnoticed.

He looked back and forth as he followed O'Neil down

further dark streets. There wasn't a single person around, yet he always felt like he was being watched. Buildings hung over him, twisting into arches, cracked windows with twitching curtains. Something scuttled past his feet and he quickly lifted his leg to find nothing below him.

Oscar hadn't noticed O'Neil had stopped, such was his distraction by his surroundings, and he almost walked straight into him.

"Listen to me, lad," O'Neil spoke. "Where we are 'bout to go is a sorry place for the likes of you. Stay close to me, and don't look at anyone. You hear?"

"Loud and clear."

O'Neil grumbled something, then made his way into a pub. Upon first impression, Oscar thought it was closed down, and imagined it would have been a delightful British pub back in the day – as it was, the door was heavy, the stink of old alcohol strong, and the sense of unwelcome immediately apparent as soon as he entered.

O'Neil nodded to the barman as he led Oscar through, who gently nodded back, stood with his arms folded and his expression dead. O'Neil opened the door to the cellar and led Oscar down. The steps were so thin, Oscar had to turn to his side in order to descend them. At their base was a small room with a small light on the far wall, and a figure hunched over in the far corner.

"Oi, Ardal," O'Neil grunted, kicking the base of something wooden, possibly a broken, discarded bench. The room was dark, with stone walls and stone floors, and a distant dripping Oscar could not place. "Wake up, you old langer."

The figure remained hunched over, shivering. Oscar assumed it was human because that was what he expected, though if someone told him it was some strange, feral, demented creature not of this world, he wouldn't be surprised.

"Ardal, stop acting the maggot, I got someone to see you."

The person turned their face, a vague illumination from the amber light coating some of their features in luminescence. Oscar peered carefully, doing his best to make this figure out.

Who on earth was this person?

"Ardal, are you hearin' me?"

The person – Ardal, as he was being referred to – turned and took a bite out of something. Oscar was sure it was a rat, but with the speed at which Ardal drew his precious food back and protected it with his body, he couldn't be sure.

"What the…" Oscar muttered, and stopped himself.

"Well, Ardal. Aren't you goin' to say hello?"

Ardal locked eyes with Oscar, and Oscar went numb. There was nothing human left behind this man. It was as if he'd been raised by animals, left to learn to distrust mankind, unused to the sound of a human voice.

"Say hello, you ungrateful sod."

Ardal slowly lifted a hand, a small gesture of greeting. His fingernails had grown half as long as the length of his finger, browned and stiff. His hand was stained with mud, flickers of red dotted across his palm.

"Ardal, are you–"

"He's here," Ardal whispered, then repeated, "He's here, he's here, he's here," in various tones, as if his voice was being spread about the room.

"This is–"

"Oscar," Ardal replied, his voice hushed. "But you're not supposed to be here… You're not supposed to be here… You're not supposed, you're not supposed, you're–"

Oscar peered intently into Ardal's eyes, intrigued but discomforted, fascinated yet mortified.

"Where am I supposed to be, Ardal?" Oscar asked.

Ardal grinned a large, lecherous grin, one that signified a thought that was filthy and impure.

"Anywhere but here," he mouthed.

"Right, that's enough," O'Neil decided. "Come on." He shoved Oscar back toward the stairs and they made their way out.

Almost as soon as they'd made their way halfway up the street away from the pub, Oscar stopped and turned to O'Neil, blurting out the question he had been waiting to have answered.

"What the hell was that?"

"That – was Ardal."

"I don't get it. Who is he? And why are you showing me him?"

O'Neil smiled. Walked closer to Oscar, close enough that Oscar could feel the warm odour of O'Neil's breath.

"He's a Sensitive," O'Neil answered.

"What?"

"You want me to spell it out for you?"

Oscar was confused. That man – that *thing* – was a Sensitive?

Sensitives were meant to be conceived by Heaven, gifts of the highest order. How could that have been a piece of something so pure, so strong?

"You ask why you should be a Sensitive for your own fate, if no one else's. You still stick by that, do you?"

"Well, yes," Oscar answered, perplexed as to the relevance. "A Sensitive is here to help other people. Not act inwardly."

O'Neil chuckled mockingly. "Yes, well that's what happens when a Sensitive don't want to be a Sensitive."

"I don't understand."

"He decided he weren't going to be a Sensitive, that such a fate weren't for him. He supressed it. In fact, he went to great lengths tryin' to suppress it – he went to see some witch doctor in Mexico, some tribe in South Africa, and other freaks on other Godforsaken continents, all with the aim of finding a way of undoing it, of making sure he never had to face up to what he was."

"I take it that didn't work."

O'Neil looked back at Oscar dumbly. "You saw him? What'd you think?"

O'Neil turned and marched on. Oscar looked over his shoulder at the pub. Lost. Wishing he could help the man somehow.

But, as he wished that, he realised how he would be helpless to do so. It slowly dawned on him how little he actually knew.

"Hurry up!" O'Neil barked, already half the street ahead.

Oscar ran to catch up.

THEN

"YOU'RE READY," FATHER HARRIS INSISTED. "YOU'RE READY, AND you need to do this yourself to figure it out. Figure out your style. This one is up to you."

Those words had run back and forth in O'Neil's mind for the entire train journey.

His style?

Did an exorcist have their own style?

Surely the prayers were the same, the gown was the same, the rosary beads, the crucifix, the Bible, all of it was the same. How does an exorcist adapt that to their own personality?

And considering that, what was O'Neil's personality?

The Church called him reckless. Said he was a loose cannon. Said his naivety was dangerous and was going to end up either getting him killed, someone else killed, or the whole world killed.

In his naivety, O'Neil had thought such comments were ridiculous.

The world?

This was a sodding child, for Christ's sake. A boy. Some pathetic little runt barely old enough to piss in a bucket, never mind do anything that could threaten the fate of the entire world.

No, he *would* do this in his style. He'd go in there and he'd batter the shit out of that demon and get it out of that kid with the venom he so ardently portrayed to those around him.

He spoke to the mother. Reassured her. Spoke to the father. Grew impatient.

All the time he was reassuring them, the ceiling above them was shaking. Dust was falling in clouds, provoked by the battering of a bed against the floor.

He knew what was at stake. Father Harris had made that perfectly clear.

Amalgamation incarnation.

Jesus, couldn't they have named it something easy? Like *cheese*. You don't want the demon to stay too long because then they will *cheese.*

Not the best example, but still better than amalgawhatsit incarwhositnow.

With a puff of his cheeks and a tap of his foot, he ended the conversation with the parents, perhaps a little curtly, and insisted that he attend to the boy.

"Would you like us in with you?" the mother asked.

Was she bloody mental? In with him? The mother witnessing her own son's bloody exorcism?

Bloody idiots, the lot of them.

"No," O'Neil answered, his expression empty, doing his best to void all detestation from his facial features. "It's probably best if I do it myself, you understand now."

"Okay," the mother confirmed, looking to her husband, holding his hand tight. "What can we do?"

"Absolutely nuttin', it's gon' get mad as a box o' frogs in there."

The mother looked uncomfortably to the father. This wasn't the answer she was expecting.

"Pray," O'Neil blurted out. It's what they wanted to hear, wasn't it? "Pray for his soul. Do your best. I'll do the rest."

"Okay," she replied, putting on her brave face. "We will. We will pray."

O'Neil turned and walked away, rolling his eyes.

Like I give a flying fuck.

The further up the stairs he walked, the colder the house grew. The door was at the end of the corridor, with smoky light pulling itself from beneath its cracks.

He opened the door to find the boy on the bed, restrained by his wrists and his ankles, the exact image suggested by the word *exorcism* – accompanied by that same smug face they always had.

Oh, if he had to see that smug face every exorcism for the rest of his life, he'd end up throttling them before he'd begun.

"Good evening, Father," the demon mocked, its voice too deep for the face before him.

It was the same as the last exorcism, and the one before that, and the one before that, and the ones before that and the million more to come after it. Cocky demon, helpless child, stupid priest. He was bored, and he wasn't even a full-fledged demon-fighter yet.

Demon-fighter. What a better name than *exorcist*. Sounds like he'd run around with guns or something, instead of a redundant container of holy water.

He took the cross on the end of his pendant from beneath his robes and let it hang on the outside of his vestment.

He kissed his amice and placed the piece of cloth adorning an image of the cross over his neck.

He took out his book: *The Rites of Exorcism.*

"Nice to see you," the demon continued. "Nice day for it?"

Yorn. This what they all did?

"We sinners," O'Neil began, "we beg you to hear us. That

RICK WOOD

you spare us, that you pardon us, that you bring us true penance."

"Where's Father Harris today?"

O'Neil stumbled momentarily. Odd that a demon should know such things. Then again, likelihood is that he'd fought this demon before, just in a different victim. He'd fought a lot of them; he was bound to meet the same one every now and then.

"That you govern and preserve your holy Church." "You on your own, priest?"

Technically, he shouldn't be. He should have waited for the person who was meant to assist to arrive. He just could not be bothered to talk to those insufferable parents any longer.

"That you preserve our Holy Father."

"This boy is mine."

"That you deliver this servant of God."

"He's not your servant anymore."

"And lead us not into temptation."

"How's your daughter?"

He stopped.

Faltered.

He shouldn't listen. He knew not to listen.

This is what demons did.

Exorcisms could take hours, days, weeks, even months and years on some occasions. He had to be patient. He'd only just started.

But patience was bloody aggravating.

"Because in this distress you have rescued me. No, wait…"

He'd got it wrong.

He'd said the prayers in the wrong order. These were just bits and pieces of various prayers.

What was he even doing?

Aw, shit.

He rummaged through the pages.

"What's the matter, priest?"

He ignored it.

"Is it because I mentioned Aubrey?"

O'Neil's eyes widened. He looked up, finally meeting the demon's eyes with his.

"I'll take her next," the demon stated.

"The hell you will."

The demon laughed. "I will take Aubrey, and I will claw her apart from the inside."

"No."

Stop listening, you're better than this.

"I will fuck her step-dad with her body."

"Shut up."

"I will fuck her mum's corpse with–"

O'Neil dumped his book; he didn't need *The Rites of Exorcism* anymore. He leapt upon the bed, taking the child's throat with his hands, squeezing hard against the oesophagus, watching the demon choke, the boy choke, both of them choke, pushing the life out of them.

"Get out of this boy!" he screamed. "Get out of him! Get out!"

The demon grinned. As it choked, it grinned.

Then it stopped choking.

Stopped pretending.

And just grinned.

"Get out, you fucking hell beast piece o' shite! Get out!"

Behind him, the door opened.

The priest who was meant to assist stood shocked, the boy's parents behind him.

"Father O'Neil!" the priest cried.

O'Neil looked down at what he was doing.

He took his hands off the child's throat.

"Oh, Father, don't stop now... I was enjoying your touch..."

O'Neil stood off, taking a step away from the bed, staring in shock at what he'd let the demon force him into.

"Time to go, Father O'Neil," the other priest said.

"Yes, Father, time to go," the demon mocked.

O'Neil turned toward the door.

"Oh, Father."

O'Neil ignored it.

"I'll get her. I'll get Aubrey, and I'll fuck her tiny body from the inside."

O'Neil turned to lash out, but the other priest held him back.

"Come on, O'Neil, time to go!" the priest insisted.

As he made his way down the stairs, thinking over the demon's words, he saw Father Harris waiting at the front door.

"Father," O'Neil said, taken by surprise. "What are you doing here?"

"You really think I'd not be standing behind you the whole time?"

"I…"

"You never go in alone! Never!"

"But the priest was late."

"Because I told him to be!"

That's when it sunk in. Just how much he'd embarrassed himself. Embarrassed Father Harris. Disgraced what he'd been taught so far, undone all the faith everyone had in him, earnt another few years of distrust.

O'Neil looked to his mentor, disappointment so clear to see.

"Get out of this house," Harris demanded.

O'Neil obeyed.

NOW

11

CHURCHES ARE MEANT TO BE PLACES OF SALVATION. PLACES OF hope. They are meant to be where couples in love marry, where babies are blessed, and people come to sing together in the name of faith.

Those people had evidently never seen a church at night.

As O'Neil led Oscar down the nave, wandering between the pews set out with cushions for people's knees and Bibles for people's minds, he couldn't help but feel unnerved. Every step he took repeated back on him. Grand architecture curved and swooped toward him with an impressive dominance. Like everywhere O'Neil seemed to be taking Oscar, there was an emphasis on shadows, with only little pieces of moonlight allowed through the stained-glass windows.

Beyond the altar, beneath the chancel on the far side of the church, O'Neil stopped. He opened a cellar door and looked expectantly to Oscar.

Oscar peered down that cellar to a pit of darkness, then looked back at O'Neil, bemused.

"You're kidding, right?"

"What I'm about to do with you cannot be done in a church. It must be hidden from God."

Oscar hesitated, toying between curiosity and dread.

"If it needs to be hidden from God, should we be doing it?"

"You want answers, don't you?"

"I don't understand how it's hidden from God if it's in His church."

"Like I said, it's not *in* His church, it is *beneath* His church. God never looks beneath His home. Do you?"

In a strange, bizarre, odd kind of way – that made total sense.

Here goes nothing... Oscar thought, and climbed into the pit below. It was even colder than the darkened church, even damper, and unequivocally pitch-black.

O'Neil landed and withdrew a torch. With one small shaft of light, he wandered forward.

"Follow me," he grunted.

He led Oscar through a narrow corridor where the walls seemed to get narrower and narrower. By the time he reached the end, he was having to duck his head and walk sideways. Never had he felt more claustrophobic; the rocky walls were literally closing in on him, their bumps and cracks grazing his shoulders. He just kept following the small burst of light from O'Neil's torch.

Eventually, the passageway led to a small room.

"Sit," O'Neil said. "In the middle of the room."

Oscar sat in the middle of the room, his legs crossed. The floor was uneven and uncomfortable. There was an inexplicable draught, and the darkness had completely unsettled his orientation

Suddenly, he felt afraid.

"Why are we here?" Oscar asked.

"Are you scared?"

Oscar considered whether to answer honestly.

"A little bit," he admitted.

O'Neil chuckled. "No, you're not. You're terrified."

"Okay, I'm terrified. I don't really get what I'm doing here."

"I'm going to put you into a trance, Oscar. A trance that will allow you to see things. See people. Talk to them, ask them questions."

"What people?"

"People you think you need to talk to."

"These people – will they, will they be real?"

O'Neil considered this.

"What is real?" O'Neil responded.

Oscar decided not to push it.

"Putting you in this state, allowing you to see the things you can see, it is unnatural. It requires a certain amount of sacrifice."

"What do I need to sacrifice?" Oscar asked, worried about what he was going to be instructed to do next.

"Control. Something everyone wants, everyone needs – and we are all hesitant to relinquish. When you exorcise a demon, Oscar, are you in control?"

"Yes."

"*Wrong!* You are *never* in control, and believing that makes you weaker. You need to admit that the demon is the one winning, always winning – unless you know that, you will never defeat it."

Oscar was getting a headache.

"Now, your fear," O'Neil continued. "Your fear is in you, isn't it? Why?"

"I'm in a dirty room where I can't see anything and the walls are closing in on me – of course I'm scared."

"But you're not letting yourself be scared, are you?"

"Of course not, why would I?"

"Because you are scared. So why reject it?"

Oscar bowed his head and rubbed his sinus. This was getting tedious.

"Why would I allow myself to be scared? How does being scared ever help me?"

"How does denying how you truly feel help you?"

Oscar had no response.

"I need you to close your eyes. I need you to feel that fear. Let it enter you, let it spread through you, put yourself in a state of pure terror – only then will you be allowed to see what you wish to see. Talk to who you wish to talk to."

Oscar sighed.

Fine.

He closed his eyes. Shut them tight.

Be scared. Be scared. Be scared.

He willed it into himself, but nothing was forthcoming. He tried again.

Be scared. Be scared. Be scared.

Waited.

And waited.

Nope. Nothing.

"Stop *trying* to be scared, boy." O'Neil's voice came from a part of the room Oscar couldn't place. "You don't need to *try* to be scared. You *are* already scared. Just allow it."

He sighed.

Fine.

I'm scared.

He thought about the room he was in. The plummeting temperature made him shiver. He feared what the item brushing past his leg could be. He worried about what was waiting for him as he walked back through the passageway.

He wondered if there was something else in there with them.

Something evil.

And that's when he felt it.

There was something. Something sinister, something not of this world. Something hovering like a bad smell, a potent odour, clinging to the cold, clinging to his body, it was on his clothes, the prickle of the upturned hairs on his arm, the scrape of something silent subtly seeping across his skin.

What was it?

It punched his chest, sucking his insides, taking him at once, stiffening his muscles, stiffening his mind.

What was it doing to him?

He tried to move.

He wasn't in control.

Whatever it was had a hold of him and was clinging on, wrapping its claws around his psyche, gripping him in its evil embrace, punishing him with its insipid thoughts.

I'm going to die.

I'm going to be possessed.

April won't survive.

Every one of these fears, these latent insecurities, ran around his mind like children playing tag, trying to catch the thought, seeing it and not reaching it, all the time constant running, all the time constant hitting his mind bombarding his mind a strafe of worries a salvo of thoughts hitting him please won't it stop I don't want it to keep going I want it to stop it's going to get me it's getting me it's getting me it's getting me.

It's got me.

He opened his eyes.

He was somewhere else.

A blank room. No end, no beginning, no colour.

Just blank.

Empty.

Oscar looked down. His hands were there, his feet were there. He was standing.

There was a man standing across from him. A man looking

back, a knowing look upon his worn face. He seemed weary, yet fresh.

"Who are you?" Oscar asked.

"My name," the man replied, "is Edward King."

12

"You're – you're Eddie? Edward King?"

Oscar's question was answered with a gentle nod.

"But – how? How is it you?"

Eddie smiled and held his arm out, beckoning Oscar to follow.

"Come," Eddie said. "Walk with me."

Oscar followed and they walked, nowhere in particular – mostly as there was nowhere in particular to walk. The room remained plain, with absent surroundings spiralling infinitely into the distance.

Eddie found a bench, unnoticeable at first, as it was the same colour as the absent surroundings. He sat on it, indicating to Oscar to do the same.

"I can't quite believe I'm talking to you," Oscar said. "I mean, how is this even possible?"

Eddie just smiled.

"You think everything can be explained so easily?" Eddie asked.

"What do you mean?"

"You ask me how it's possible. That's the problem with

69

people. We spend too much time asking why and how, without realising how much we could never understand the answers."

"I – I still don't understand."

Eddie smiled at Oscar once more. He had an air of relaxation around him. The demeanour of someone wise but unassuming. A teacher; someone who wasn't willing to give you the answers, but let you understand them for yourself.

"Think of an ant. Can you explain to an ant why a human might stamp on them?"

"No, I guess not."

"No. But there is still an explanation, even if that ant can't understand it. Just one they'd never be able to comprehend."

"So you're saying that we're just ants?"

"No, I'm not saying we're ants. I'm saying that you are here for questions. Just don't be frustrated if you don't get the answers."

Oscar couldn't believe he was sitting next to this man.

Eddie's history was complicated at best, and most of it Oscar had heard from Derek or read in Derek's journals. Eddie was once Derek's best friend, his mentee. But there was always a question as to where Eddie had come from and why he, as an exorcist, found commanding demons so easy. Unfortunately, Derek found out the truth too late, and his best friend became his biggest enemy. The Edward King war was known as the war between mankind and the Antichrist – something brought about by this man's existence. Hell had opened up and demons had walked the Earth whilst Eddie fought himself from the inside. Eddie had been both a powerful force for good and a destructive force for evil – although only one side of him had won in the end.

"You want to know what a Sensitive is," Eddie said.

"Yeah. I guess that would be my first – and, well, my main question."

"But you already know the answer."

"I…" Oscar thought – well, yes, there was an obvious answer. "Someone who's been conceived by Heaven. You were the first of our time."

Eddie smiled knowingly, but it wasn't arrogant – in fact, it had an unmistakable air of charm. "Wrong twice, I'm afraid."

"How do you mean?"

Eddie inhaled a deep breath, even though he didn't breathe. "If your definition of a Sensitive is someone who's been conceived by Heaven, then I would not be the first of modern times. That would be Martin."

"Of course, you were–"

"Conceived by Hell."

"But it didn't define you. I mean, in the end, you had a piece of Heaven in you, and it won out."

"Yes." Eddie laughed. "Because of luck. Because of good timing. Because I was surrounded by people willing to fight for my soul – a soul being something the devil had completely underestimated the power of. Don't forget, I killed many souls before I was stopped."

"What about the second thing?"

"I beg your pardon?"

"You said I was wrong about two things. What was the other thing?"

"Ah, yes. Your definition of a Sensitive. That one has been conceived by Heaven."

"Isn't that true?"

"Well, I suppose by the logic I'm going to give you, I could have been the first Sensitive when you think about it. Because a Sensitive needn't have necessarily been conceived by Heaven in order to do the things they can do."

"You mean, we could have been conceived by…"

Eddie nodded. "Hell, that's right."

Oscar's head dropped. This changed his entire world. His

entire outlook. The way he perceived the existence of him and those closest to him.

"And if I was conceived by Hell, could I – could I end up like you did? Killing your friends, destroying everything?"

"If one was to be conceived by Hell, it would almost be a certainty."

"And how do you know? How do you know if you're conceived by Hell, and not Heaven?"

Eddie lifted his arms in a shrugging motion.

"Please, you've got to give me more than that. There must be a way to know."

"There is."

"And what is it?"

"Once you've turned into a demonic beast and killed all those people you love – including April. That's when you know."

Oscar shook his head. What was Eddie suggesting?

What did Eddie think Oscar was going to do?

"But – but I can't, I can't let myself. I can't be, I don't feel it in me."

"You think it can't be you?"

"No. I don't feel Hell within me."

"But you have turned into something evil before, haven't you? You have tried killing those you love. Including April."

Oscar shook his head harder.

"That's because I was under the control of something!"

"And how did something manage to control you so easily? If you're so pure, so made of Heaven, how was the link so simple?"

"No, I can't be."

"You might not be. There's no way to know for certain."

"Surely you can tell?"

"No, that wouldn't be right."

"Why not?"

"Because I'm dead. It's not my place to interfere with the living."

"But you're interfering with the living right now!"

Eddie stood.

"I'm sorry my thoughts weren't the thoughts you wished to hear. But you came here for answers, and I have endeavoured to give you what you needed."

"But I have more questions. There is more I need to know."

Eddie placed a reassuring hand on Oscar's shoulder.

"You'll come back here again. We'll speak more. When you're ready. When O'Neil thinks it's time. Then, I will have more answers. For now, just go home. Get some sleep. Consider what you've learnt."

Oscar went to speak, but his words fell short.

Eddie backed away until he was nothing. Gone. Faded into the emptiness of the room.

Oscar was left standing there until his eyes opened and he was back in the dirty, dank room, with O'Neil staring at him.

13

OSCAR DIDN'T SAY A WORD FOR THE ENTIRE WALK HOME.

O'Neil didn't seem to mind. In fact, it seemed like he relished it. The longer the silence was prolonged, the more vigour there was to his walking. His strides opened up and his pace increased and, despite being considerably older than Oscar, Oscar found himself having to hurry to catch up.

In the end, Oscar gave up and let O'Neil march on ahead. Edinburgh felt like one giant hill. As they left the dark, dismal streets of their day and entered the bustling streets of Edinburgh at night, he remembered how much he actually liked this city. Even though he'd been exposed to the dodgy parts, he knew that was something every city kept as a dirty little secret. As it was, people didn't barge into him, and that made it unlike any other city he'd been to.

Strange, really. In the past few months he'd searched the world, explored different countries, and ended up sleeping on the streets of Rome. As it was, it was a city a four-hour train journey from April that would give him his answers.

April.

Oh, April.

Eddie's words repeated, fighting against any thoughts that Oscar used in an attempt to reassure himself.

Until now, he'd managed to convince himself that his part in what had happened between him and April was the result of his faux-daughter's control. The demon that had taken control of him.

Something that could happen to anyone.

Even a Sensitive.

But that denial was starting to crumble. Truth was starting to burst into his life and he didn't like it. He wasn't sure if he wanted to learn any more.

Could he be like Eddie?

Could he be a creature of Hell, rather than Heaven?

If he ever went home – would he be a danger to April?

He surprised himself. This whole time he'd begun many thoughts with *when I go home...*

This was the first time that sentence had begun with *if.*

They reached O'Neil's house and entered without a word spoken. Oscar slumped on the sofa in his catatonic state, and O'Neil disappeared to the kitchen then reappeared moments later with two tumblers of whiskey, one for himself and one for Oscar.

Oscar wasn't really a whiskey guy. He liked a beer, but whiskey was always so sharp. It made him flinch every time he took it.

In that moment, he downed it like water.

"Another," he said, handing O'Neil back the glass.

O'Neil smiled, as if they were finally sharing something in common, and hurriedly returned from the kitchen with another. This time, Oscar sipped it.

"So I take it you didn't get good news, then?" O'Neil asked.

Oscar didn't know what to say. How to answer. There was

nothing he could offer that would reassure himself or confirm the hypothesis.

Instead, he just went with a direct, gentle, "I think I'm going to go to bed."

"Okay, right you are, kid," O'Neil said. "Be ready early in the morning, I got something else I want to show you."

Something else?

Oscar felt like objecting, but he didn't have the energy. Besides, this was what he came here for. Did he think it was going to be simple? That someone was going to be waiting there to say, *Yes, being a Sensitive is wonderful, giving you a long, happy life, a rich array of relationships, and zero complications whatsoever.*

No.

This was the truth he expected.

He lay down on the bed and took out his phone. He'd lost his old one a while ago and had needed to get a new one, meaning that no one had his number. But he had theirs.

In a wave of nostalgic desire, Oscar felt a deep craving to hear April's voice, if only for a second.

He gave in.

He dialled April's number and put the phone to his ear.

It rang.

He waited.

Then, there it was. Her clear, unmistakable voice, a voice that made his heart race, better than he'd remembered.

"Hello?"

Oscar closed his eyes. Savoured it. This was all he had, and it wasn't much, but it meant a lot.

"Hello?" she prompted.

He went to speak, then thought against it.

She didn't need him back. Not yet.

If ever.

"Hello, is anyone there?"

He hung up.

Dropped the phone.

Closed his eyes and replayed the call in his mind, again and again, and again, and again. Her voice, clear as if it was right beside him, defiantly hers.

He fell asleep with its beauty cascading through his dreams.

THEN

DEATH.

Debilitation.

Illness.

Just a sample of the list of possibilities firing through O'Neil's thoughts.

It was like a game show where they displayed all the prizes on a conveyer belt – except instead of a conveyer belt, it was his mind; and instead of prizes, there were just more awful possibilities, each one worse than the last.

Natasha would not have called him unless she was desperate. Unless there was something she could not solve without him.

Her husband opened the door. It was the last person he expected to see. He'd spent so much time worrying about his daughter, he hadn't even considered what he'd say should he meet the man who falsely believed he was Aubrey's father – the guy who had no idea whatsoever that his wife had had a brief affair with a priest.

"Hi, my name is Tony," the husband said, offering his hand,

which O'Neil automatically shook. "Thank you for coming. This way."

Tony stood back and allowed O'Neil into the house. O'Neil sauntered warily through the hallway, inspecting photos of Aubrey as a baby, as a toddler, first school photo, a family photo with her mummy and... Tony.

O'Neil found himself slowly entering the living room, where Natasha sat on the edge of the sofa, her face covered in her hands, tears running over her cheeks, trailing down the space where other tears had dried.

"Oh, Nat," O'Neil said, sitting down next to her, putting an arm around her.

Tony appeared in the doorway, but O'Neil ignored him. He wouldn't suspect there was any history. All he would see was the local priest comforting one of his parishioners.

"Nat, come on, look at me."

She shook her head. Refuted his request. Buried her head further into her arms, running her hands through her greasy hair.

"Nat," O'Neil insisted, pulling away her arms. She resisted, at first. But he tugged, and she gave way, and what he found was a distraught face with flickers of anger aimed in his direction.

"How dare you!" she whispered.

"What?"

"You brought this in here! You did it! You brought it in!"

"Now, now, dear," Tony said, completely unwanted by both O'Neil and Natasha. "There's no way to know that. He's just here to be of some help."

"Oh, Tony, would you just–" She paused, not knowing what she was about to request. "Could you – could you get the father some tea?"

Tony nodded and left the room.

82

O'Neil kept his hand on her back, a gesture of reassurance – but he daren't put his arm back around her.

"Talk to me," O'Neil said. "Tell me. Tell me what it is."

"It's… it's Aubrey."

"Is she okay? Is she hurt? What happened to her?"

Natasha shook her head at him, as if she knew something he didn't, and that knowledge was repulsing her.

"You have no idea, do you?" she said.

"No idea of what?"

"Aren't you an exorcist? Shouldn't you feel this kind of thing happening? Especially with your own daughter?"

"What, you – you think she's possessed? Come on, Nat, you sure you aren't being farfetched?"

"Me? Aren't you the one who does this for a living?"

"Yes, but in most cases, demonic possession isn't the case. It is, in fact, very rare. In most cases, a psychiatrist can diagnose a mental health condition, and that's the better option of treatment." She said nothing. "Have you done that? Have you taken her to a psychiatrist?"

"What do you think, you idiot?" she snapped.

He nodded. "Okay. And what did they say?"

"Oh, what they all say. Schizophrenia, psychosis, blah blah blah. They don't have a clue. They are just waving terms around and hoping one sticks."

"And why are you so sure they are wrong?"

"Let me ask you a question, Connor. In all these cases of misinterpreted possession, all of these cases that should be mental health – have any of those victims managed to levitate items off the ground?"

"Some have seizures that may seem–"

"No. Levitate items off the ground. As in, pick up a bookcase without moving and throw it at me."

O'Neil took a moment. He wasn't sure what to make of it. In his experience, people interpret things however their mind chooses to. Exorcism, whilst it kept him busy, was a rare commodity. It wasn't something you diagnosed without looking at all the factors in great detail. And this included whether or not the mother had thought something like a bookcase was being thrown at her.

He'd seen it before. Skewed perceptions.

"Tell you what," she said, her voice low and particular, enunciating every syllable. "If you do not believe me, if you think I am crazy – why don't you go see for yourself?"

He sighed.

If that's what it took.

"Fine."

He stood. Straightened his collar. Walked into the corridor.

"Here's your tea, Father," Tony said, appearing at his side.

"Please, I'll have it in the living room – I won't be a moment."

"Right you are." Tony took the tea into the living room.

O'Neil placed his foot on the bottom step and was hit with an overwhelming feeling of nostalgia. The last time he was climbing these steps, Natasha was half-stripped, and his lips were pressed against hers so hard it was like they were fighting.

As he stepped onto the upstairs landing, the temperature plummeted. A symptom, yes, but he still kept his scepticism.

He walked through the hallway to the room with a playful sign on the door that read *Aubrey*.

He opened it, and found his daughter laying soundly on the bed. Her face was pale, her breathing deep and croaking, the furniture upturned.

He moved a wicker chair from the corner of the room and sat next to the girl.

"Hello, Aubrey," O'Neil said, feeling a pang in his chest, a sense of loss, knowledge that he was sitting opposite what was missing from his life. Did she really have no idea that she was looking into the eyes of her true father? "How are you?"

The girl smiled. A strange, discomforting smile, but nothing not of this world.

"Do you know who I am?"

"Father," Aubrey spoke.

"Yes, I am a father. I'm a priest at the church by the–"

"No… my father."

O'Neil shook himself out of it, positive that he didn't hear correctly.

"Sorry, what did you say?"

"You are my father."

"I – I am not your father."

"No, that's right. You are *Aubrey's* father."

O'Neil closed his eyes, gathered himself, then readdressed the girl.

"And what would make you say that?"

A new kind of smile spread across the girl's face, a sneaky smile, a sinister smile.

"I told you I'd take her next," it said.

NOW

15

A MENTAL INSTITUTION.

A ruddy mental institution.

"Oh, Father, you take me to all the nicest places," Oscar joked. His joke was met with silence, but he had expected nothing more.

To be honest, he wondered why he was even surprised he was there. O'Neil had so far taken him to a dirty, hidden room beneath a church and a cellar beneath a pub where everyone looked like they wanted to kill him.

So, by that logic – why wouldn't O'Neil take him to a mental institution? It seems perfectly logical, doesn't it?

Here we bloody go again.

"Come on," O'Neil barked. "We haven't got much time."

Oscar wondered what it was they didn't have much time for, but decided against asking. The question would either be met with silence, an irritable remark, or an answer he didn't want to hear. Oscar was learning fairly quickly just to keep his mouth shut.

O'Neil spoke to a receptionist who gave him the nod and pointed down the corridor.

"Yes, yes, I know the way," O'Neil grumbled, and darted down the corridor, not even looking back to see if Oscar was following.

The stereotype of a mental institution is of a building full of absentminded madness, demented souls wandering around either overly dormant, or so manic they need to be restrained. Paint would crack off the walls, nurses would look tired, and the whole place would be neglected by society.

This was a very old stereotype that simply wasn't the case anymore.

When someone is sectioned, they are moved into a mental health facility for help. They are placed in the care of someone that can help them with their diagnosis, and the places are not as derelict as one would have expected decades ago.

Despite this, the more Oscar walked through the institution, the more it seemed like he was walking back in time. The building started out as a well put together facility, with doctors who smiled at you and patients who were striving to get better. There were posters adorning the walls with positive, inspirational quotes, and open rooms for patients where they were allowed books and posters of their own.

Yet, the farther Oscar followed O'Neil, the more the corridor seemed to be disintegrating. With each double door they walked through, the nurses looked paler and the walls became more decrepit – by the time they reached the room and O'Neil turned toward him, Oscar was shivering, rubbing his arms for warmth.

"You do exactly as I say, when I say it, d'you hear?"

Oscar nodded.

O'Neil entered a code into the door, opened it, and allowed Oscar through. Once that door was closed, it was only another few paces until there was another door O'Neil entered a code for.

Oscar wondered what could be so bad that they required a two-door entry.

O'Neil led Oscar into a small room, a dank room with sickly cream walls. Along one of the walls was a window.

As Oscar looked through the window, his breath stopped. He choked. He willed himself to look away, but he couldn't.

Three men. Each on a separate bed. Each with a straight-jacket wrapped around them, their ankles and waist attached to chains that fed through metal loops beside their mattress. Despite their many restraints, they didn't spend a single second being still. They wriggled with such ferocity, their beds had also been tied down. In the eyes of these three men were bloodshot, fully dilated, red pupils. Their hair stuck on end in greasy waves, their faces scarred with remnants of what looked like fingernails, and their voices – oh, their voices. Multiple voices, each in pain, each wailing in terror, mixing into a crescendo of agonising horror, screeching and grinding and moaning and spewing and making Oscar want to run for the door.

O'Neil watched Oscar's face. Studying him.

"Why aren't we helping them?" Oscar asked.

"I knew that'd be your first question," was the only reply he got.

"Well, why aren't we?"

O'Neil gazed upon the three squirming, relentlessly struggling men before him.

"They used to be my friends," O'Neil said. "They were all brilliant exorcists. And Sensitives."

Oscar turned to O'Neil with a flicker of anger. What was the point O'Neil was trying to make?

"Why is it always Sensitives in pain that you show me?"

"Because this was their inevitable fate."

Oscar scoffed and shook his head.

"Every time you perform an exorcism," O'Neil continued, "you open yourself up that little bit more to evil, and it leaves a mark. A piece of vulnerability. And you commit these acts, even though you're most vulnerable – it's like putting your king on the front line. What better target is there than an exorcist – the world's protection against the corrupt?"

"You're trying to say this is how I'll end up?"

"Your ending hasn't been written yet, but you'll have felt it, I'm sure. That piece of your goodness that gets chipped away with each confrontation you have with a demon. Most exorcists end their lives in a spiral into supernatural madness. You think you'll be any different?"

Neither of them said anything for a long few minutes. They each stared at the three struggling victims before them. Oscar noticed how they barely blinked. Their eyes were always wide open, always in pain.

He wanted to do something.

If they used to be exorcists, or Sensitives, surely that was even more reason to help. Surely that was more reason to do whatever it took to free them.

"I want to perform an exorcism," Oscar declared.

O'Neil snorted with laughter.

"You don't have to be involved if you don't want to," Oscar insisted. "But I wish to perform one anyway. If they used to be one of us, then that gives us all the more–"

"That's your solution to everything, isn't it? An exorcism?"

"To demonic possession, yes."

"Understandable. You want to help, and it's the only solution you know. It's like putting a plaster on a cut. But what if not every cut needed a plaster?"

"I have no idea what you're on about."

O'Neil shook his head, inhaled.

"You ever heard of something called amalgamation incarnation?"

Oscar shook his head. What was this guy on about?

"No," he said irritably. "No, I haven't. Why don't you share the knowledge with me, hm?"

"What do you think we're fighting for? If a demon will just latch onto another human soul once the exorcism has been a success, then why bother? What is it we are saving these people from?"

Oscar shrugged. "Pain?"

"No. Time."

Oscar waited for more explanation. He grew impatient.

"Time?" Oscar prompted.

"A demon latches onto a human's soul because it wants to take that human's place on the Earth. It wants to banish that person from its body so it can wreak its own kind of havoc. So what if that demon succeeds? Could you exorcise it then?"

"I'd at least try."

O'Neil shook his head. "Stop being so foolish. Amalgamation incarnation is when the demon has latched onto a soul for so long, has been in the body for such a length of time, that it has entwined itself with that soul. It has now taken that body. That demon has taken that place on Earth and that person is no more. It has amalgamated."

"So an exorcism–"

"Would be pointless. You're no longer fighting a demon out of a body. You're just fighting the demon. The person is gone. You can't cast someone out of their own skin."

Oscar looked back at the three former exorcists, writhing against their restraints – only this time, he did it with a new perception. A new awareness. And new sympathy.

"So they are hopeless?"

"Yes."

"Why don't we put them out of their misery?"

O'Neil chuckled that arrogant, annoying chuckle Oscar was starting to detest. "How about you go in there and try?"

Oscar went to object, then stopped. He finally understood.

This was what happened when the hopelessness became reality.

Some people, Oscar was beginning to understand, could just not be saved.

16

THE JOURNEY BENEATH THE CHURCH, TO THE ROOM HIDDEN from Heaven, was only a little less eerie than the last time. At least Oscar knew what to expect, even if he still had no idea where he was going.

Falling into the trance hadn't been any tougher. In order to fall back in, he'd had to access his fear once more, and his fear went deeper than just the darkness of the room and the absence of control.

It was everything.

The thought of returning home.

Of what the true origins of his gift (as it was so often referred to) could be.

Whether he was going to hurt everyone he loved.

And April.

Oh, April.

He saw her in his mind as clear as if she was standing in front of him. Her eyes beseeching him to stay. Her strength covering the weakness that his leaving had caused.

He missed the calm touch of her hand, the soft reassurance of her voice, the comfort of her smile.

But what if he was going to destroy that?

The image of her grew grainy. April cried out to him, a claw swiping up her chest, her throat; she was on her knees, crying, suffering, begging, suffering, praying, reaching out for him to stop, my chest, just stop please my chest hurts just let her go you love her my chest don't you don't you love her why would do this why would–

And there he was, in the absent room. Vacancy as far as his eyes could see. A distant nothing casting vague light over the room.

"Hello again," Eddie said.

Oscar turned. There he was. The man himself once again, as if he had always been there, waiting for him.

"Hi," Oscar replied, eyeing Eddie cautiously.

"What's the matter?" Eddie asked.

"I don't know," Oscar said, not sure why he was suddenly so on edge. "I guess the last time I saw you, you kind of gave me some bad news."

"I didn't give you any news, Oscar. I just gave you thoughts. Shall we?"

Eddie indicated the same bench that they had sat on last time.

Again, Oscar had reservations, but wasn't sure why. After pausing, he reluctantly sat next to Eddie.

"What is it you're so worried about?" Eddie asked.

"I don't know. I guess the idea that being a Sensitive might mean that I hurt my friends."

"Your friends? Or your girlfriend?"

Oscar looked down.

"I almost killed her before," he said.

"And you could almost kill her again."

Oscar frowned, peering at Eddie.

"Aren't you meant to be reassuring?"

"Is that what you want? Reassurance?"

Oscar stood, began meandering away from the bench, his hands in his pockets, aimlessly sauntering.

"Why did you come here, Oscar?" Eddie asked, standing.

"I don't know. You have all the answers, why don't you tell me?"

"I killed people, Oscar. I killed my best friend, the woman who meant more to me than anything. Because I let myself get comfortable, because I never thought it would really happen. Shouldn't you be prepared for any eventuality?"

"And then what? I separate myself off from the world, hide myself away so I don't hurt anyone? I end up like Father O'Neil, or Martin, or like all the other once-great Sensitives I've seen? Is that what I'm supposed to do?"

"What do you think you're supposed to–"

"Stop that!" Oscar stood, throwing his arms in the air. "It seems like every time I make a comment or ask another question you just reply with some other stupid question. Why don't you tell me something useful? Huh?"

"Okay." Eddie stood also, stepping toward him. "No one is safe from you. No one."

Oscar had nothing to say. Was this the answer he was searching for? That him being alive caused danger to others?

"Surely you'd know," Oscar thought aloud. "Surely you would know if someone was conceived by Heaven or by Hell. Surely, with who you are–"

"Who I am?"

"Yes, with who you are – surely you could tell me. Or someone could. I mean, how did you know?"

"Okay. I knew because I afflicted pain on those around me without being aware. Because I killed small animals for pleasure without being at all in control. This is all what happened leading up to me becoming what I was."

Oscar shook his head. He couldn't take this any longer.

"I was under the influence of a demon!"

"And I wasn't? Just because the demon was inside of me, you think it was any better?"

"I want out. I want to get out. I want to go back."

"Why, Oscar?"

Oscar peered around himself, lifting his arms in the air, looking for a way out, frantically searching.

"Let me out! I want to go back! I want to go back!"

"Oscar–"

"Somebody! Just snap me out of it!"

"Oscar–"

"Just let me out!"

"Oscar–"

Oscar paused his shouting.

The final mention of his name.

The voice was different. It was older, gruffer, deeper, it was…

He turned.

Eddie was gone.

There stood Derek.

"Derek?"

"Oscar, you need to listen to me, we haven't much time."

"What's going on?"

"Oscar, you're in danger."

"What? What danger?"

"Oscar, listen, none of this is–"

Oscar's eyes shot open.

He was back in the pitch-black room, O'Neil standing before him with a torchlight.

"Well?" O'Neil asked. "Did you find your answers?"

17

THE GENTLE AROMA OF COFFEE PROVED A WELCOME RELIEF. Around the café, various couples and friends and families shared a moment, all melding into the gentle ambience of quiet chatter.

Oscar was sat alone. He relished it.

For some reason, he thought getting away from O'Neil would be difficult – but when Oscar said he was going to go find a local café to collect his thoughts and would rather be left to his solitude, O'Neil had practically jumped at the opportunity. No sooner had Oscar finished his sentence than O'Neil had reeled off a number of local coffee shops Oscar could go to.

Oscar hadn't taken a note of any of them. He just went for a walk, drifting through Edinburgh, across the Meadows, until he found somewhere small. An independent chain, possibly family owned – one where he wouldn't be bothered by the hustle and bustle that you'd get in a recognised brand.

He did nothing but stir his coffee with his teaspoon and take gentle sips every now and then. No maps, no phone calls to the Vatican, no desperate searching, no quibbles, no issues, nothing – just calmness. Hoping he could somehow find a way to be peaceful and calm.

In truth, nothing could be tougher.

He stared absentmindedly at the napkin discarded without thought upon the table, but he saw other images.

Derek.

What was he going to say?

Why was he there?

And, where was *there* exactly?

Where had O'Neil put him – and how had his fears directed his way? It only dawned on him now how unusual that seemed. Why would somewhere good be found through focussing on one's fear?

But if it wasn't good – how was Edward King there?

Oscar rubbed his hand through his hair. He was getting a headache. He paid his bill and meandered out into the street. A large group of schoolchildren bustled past him, tiny people with high-vis waistcoats all joined in a long line by hands, led by reluctant, ill-tempered teachers.

He found his way to a bench and sat, watching the world as it went about its business, no one knowing or caring what lurked beneath.

He came here after answers, but it felt like more answers just led to more questions.

Then again, had he really come to look for answers? If he had to be honest with himself, the one thing he'd been seeking more than anything else was reassurance. Something that told him what had happened with their child – *no, not my 'child'* – with their *demon*… That it was a fluke. A freak occurrence. Something that would never repeat itself. He had to know there was no way he would ever be able to harm April again.

If anything, he was learning that harming those he loved could even be his purpose.

No.

Stop it.

That can't be what Eddie was getting at.

Maybe Eddie was just proposing thoughts, was playing devil's advocate.

Of course, he'd been the devil's advocate before.

And Derek.

What about Derek?

Oscar, listen, none of this is –

What?

None of this was what?

Right? True? Meant to hurt him?

"You all right, hun?" came the voice of a soft Scottish accent.

"Huh?" Oscar grunted, looking up at an attractive woman standing over him, long, brown hair and piercing green eyes. Once he saw her, he wished he'd had a more articulate response.

"You just look a bit stressed, that's all. Are you okay?"

Was he okay?

Was he bloody okay?

"Yeah, I'm fine," he lied. "Just, things on my mind, you know?"

"That happens."

Oscar looked for a coffee in his hands and realised he hadn't got one. Instead, his hands met and his fingers played with each other.

"Do you mind if I sit next to you? There aren't really any other free benches."

She smiled a million-dollar smile at him.

It's so simple. Isn't it?

You see a pretty woman, they smile at you, and suddenly, you think you're in love.

Could Oscar ever be in love with anyone but April?

He didn't believe in soulmates, that was for sure. He believed there wasn't anyone destined to be with him.

But he believed in April.

"Sure," Oscar said, sounding more impatient than he felt.

"My name is Hazel," she said, taking a seat next to him and opening a shop-bought egg and cress sandwich.

"Oscar."

"So what's troubling you?"

Oscar smiled at such a ridiculous scenario. Why on Earth was this stranger just approaching him and asking him to share his troubles? It felt like the opening to a really bad romcom.

"Why are you so sure something is troubling me?"

"'Cause it's obvious. Is it girls?" Hazel asked.

"Ah, no. No girl problems here."

"Tell me."

"I don't know you."

"Yeah, you do. I'm Hazel, remember?"

Oscar laughed into his fidgeting hands.

"I just have a lunch hour to kill, I'm bored, I'm lonely, and you look really sad. So, help me kill an hour. What's up?"

"What's up?"

"I'm good with problems."

"Well, I don't know. You're probably not too good with these ones."

"Try me."

Oscar went to speak, and fumbled over forming a coherent answer.

"I just – I'm a bit lost at the moment."

"Lost as in, you don't know where this is, or lost as in, life?"

"The latter."

"Well, I heard it's best not to overthink it. We are who we are, and we all end up as that person eventually. Don't you think?"

Oh, if only she knew what the problem was, she'd realise that was the worst piece of advice anyone had ever given.

"Yeah, I guess."

"See! Problem solved. Anything else I can help with while I'm here?"

Oscar chuckled politely. "Ah, no, I think I'm all set."

"Do you live around here?"

"No, I'm"–he went to say *on holiday*, then realised how wrong that would actually be–"I'm not from around here. I'm just staying a little while."

"On your own?"

"Pretty much."

"Well, if you would like some company tonight, you're welcome to come join me for dinner."

"Oh, I don't know about that."

"Oh, come on. It's with my family, so it's nothing wild – but my two brothers and my sister are all married and with kids, so I'm always tagged on the end next to the dog. If I had a plus one, it would make my evening more interesting. Think of it as doing me a favour! After all, I just solved all your life problems, you owe me…"

Oscar smiled. A family dinner. Imagine. It felt just so… normal. Something Oscar wasn't used to.

"I think I'll have to pass."

"Oh, how come? You have a girlfriend?"

"Yes, actually."

"Well this isn't a marriage proposal, Oscar. It's just a dinner, just a bit of company. You look too miserable to be left on your own."

Oscar said nothing.

"Well," she decided, pulling out a pen, grabbing Oscar's arm and writing on it "Here's the address. Come at seven o'clock if you change your mind."

Oscar looked at the words scribbled beneath his wrist.

"It was nice to meet you, Oscar. I hope you find what you're looking for."

"It was nice to meet you too, Hazel."

And with a cute smile, Hazel returned to the crowd of strangers, and Oscar went back to his solitude.

He'd enjoyed that conversation.

It had been a nice break from his thoughts.

THEN

18

"GOD, WHOSE NATURE IS EVER MERCIFUL!" O'NEIL SCREAMED; screamed like he'd never screamed before. "Accept our prayer that this servant of Yours, bound by the fetters of sin, may be pardoned by Your loving kindness!"

Below him, his unknowing daughter, Aubrey. Her childish body having been made to do unchildish things, squirming, writhing over the floor, turning and clenching and screaming and begging.

O'Neil had been at it for forty hours straight.

And he would go another forty hours if need be.

His body felt empty. His mind felt gone. His eyes dry, his stomach acidic, and his resolve unbeaten.

He was toward the end of the exorcism and he knew it. He felt it. He'd done enough to know when he was winning, when the demon would give in soon, when the disgusting beast that dwelled within was on its last legs, its last tries, and its last grasp on the poor child of God it had devoured.

They had been in every room of the house chasing this demon as it tried to get away, with Natasha and Tony chasing, blocking the exits, restraining when they could, keeping the thing inside.

Now it was stuck. Stuck on the floor of the family room, its belly in the air, its bleeding crotch rising to the sky. Her face had been practically ripped to shreds, her body covered in wounds, and every new mark O'Neil saw the demon make was another new mark on his soul.

But he wasn't ever prepared to let this one go. He would fight to the very end.

Now for the final prayer.

Tony and Aubrey stood aside.

Every item in the room had been flung from one wall to the other, smashed, destroyed. But now the floating objects rested, and all that was left was O'Neil and the struggling body of the girl.

"And now, demon, I speak directly to you."

The demon let out a long, painful moan, multiple pitches; and Aubrey's voice was definitely amongst them.

"I command you, unclean spirit, whoever you are, along with all your minions now attacking this servant of God."

He held out his cross, held it until his fingers bled, its edges digging into his palm, his faith strong, his mind stronger.

"Your daughter… is mine…" were the last helpless cries of the beast.

"By the mysteries of the incarnation," O'Neil persisted, undeterred by its torment, unperturbed by its lies, "passion and resurrection and ascension of our Lord Jesus Christ, I, who am minister of God despite my unworthiness, shall not let you embolden in harm this or any other servant of His!"

"I… am… no… servant…"

Its sickening roar pushed O'Neil back against the wall.

Determined to resist, he dove upon Aubrey, mounted her infantile body and pressed the cross against her forehead, watching it smoke, hearing the tinge as it burned.

"They shall lay their hands upon the sick and all will be well with them!"

The demon twisted Aubrey's head to Tony, who stood with his hands over his mouth, just like his wife.

"Did you know?" the demon asked.

"May Jesus, son of Mary, Lord and Saviour of the world, empower me!"

"That... this girl... is his..."

"Through the merits and intercession of His holy apostles, Peter and Paul, and His saints – I will show you no mercy!"

The demon screamed, cackled, balled the girl's hands into fists, tried to resist, helplessly fought against the prayers.

"I command you, demon – leave this girl!"

Her voice sung out over the painful screams.

"I command you – leave this servant of God!"

Aubrey could be heard crying. Somewhere in there, she was crying.

"I command you – leave my daughter!"

Tony looked to Natasha, who couldn't look back. His mind full of questions, but for now, he was too full of relief.

Because she was back.

Aubrey was back.

It was her face again. Her poor, helpless, tear-ridden face.

Crying.

O'Neil stood and backed away.

Aubrey reached out to her mother. Her face drenched with tears, she reached out.

"Mum!"

"Oh, my darling!"

Natasha enveloped her daughter in her arms and held her tight. Tony joined them.

O'Neil leant against the windowsill. He wiped sweat from his face. As his body finally relaxed, he realised just how weary he was.

But sleep could wait.

She was back.

His daughter was back.

"Thank you!" Natasha cried out to O'Neil. "Thank you so much!"

And for the longest time they stayed as they were. Natasha, Tony, and Aubrey stuck in a suffocating embrace.

O'Neil watching on from the other side of the room.

Eventually, Aubrey lifted her head and turned to O'Neil. Her face a mixture of relief and confusion.

"Thank you," she said.

O'Neil smiled. "You're welcome."

Aubrey looked to her mother, to Tony, then to O'Neil.

"Is it true?" she asked.

"What?" O'Neil replied.

"That you're my father? Is it true what it said?"

O'Neil bowed his head. Paused. Gathered his thoughts. Looked to Natasha, still hugging her daughter, still rubbing her hair and kissing her forehead. To Tony, who looked back, waiting just as eagerly for an answer.

"No, I'm not–"

"Yes," Natasha interrupted. "Yes, he is."

Tony leant back, not knowing what to say.

O'Neil didn't care about Tony.

His daughter knew.

She finally knew.

And he had so much love to share with her.

"Then how – how could you do this to me?" Aubrey asked.

"What?" O'Neil responded.

"You put this demon in me. It was your fault."

"Darling," Natasha tried. "He saved you from it."

"But it wouldn't have been there if it weren't for him."

Just like that, O'Neil's hope left. His world shattered and fell

QUESTIONS FOR THE DEVIL

away from him. The moment he'd dreamt of, the opportunity he'd desired, gone in an instant.

Aubrey never spoke to him again.

Ever.

Tony continued as her dad. Somehow, he and Natasha worked past it, and that was how they continued in their life. Like nothing had ever changed.

O'Neil distanced himself. Waited for the day his daughter changed her mind. Until the day she grew old enough to want to know her real father and she came knocking on his door to find him, and he could say how much he loved her, how much she meant.

But that day never came.

To O'Neil and Aubrey, it was as if he was dead.

No, worse.

It was as if he'd never existed.

NOW

OSCAR WASN'T SURE WHETHER IT WAS OUT OF CURIOSITY, wonder, or just sheer loneliness that he was turning up at this address. But, as seven o'clock arrived, he found himself lingering on the edge of the street, walking back and forth, unable to decide whether he was coming or going.

It was clear which house Hazel had invited him to – it was the one with all the cars parked outside.

That meant there were a lot of people.

Strange, really – large social situations had never scared Oscar before. Then again, he'd always had April with him when he had to face them. Now, on his own, the idea of walking into a house full of people he didn't know and having to engage in forced, awkward conversation made him shudder.

He watched as another car pulled up. A man stepped out, followed by a woman, followed by a young girl and boy. An older couple walked out of the door and the two children went running up to them. They hoisted them up like grandparents do, holding them and swinging them and, though Oscar couldn't hear them, he had no doubt that there were comments about how much they'd grown.

Hazel appeared. Hugged the two children, the couple, and ushered them in. As everyone else went back inside, Hazel loitered for a moment, looking around. Checking to see if someone was there, someone she was expecting.

Oscar took a step back, so he was in the shadow of the house farthest along the street.

Hazel gave up and went back inside.

Right, Oscar told himself.

Decision time.

Either go in and say hello, or leave and stop being a creep. There was a neighbourhood watch sign on the lamppost above his head, and people would no doubt be twitching their curtains and wondering who this strange man was.

He took a deep breath and walked with purpose, directly toward the house.

As he did, the window to the living room came into view, and the hive of people became visible.

Oscar slowed down.

Inside, he saw numerous children running about. They were talking keenly to their grandparents, some of them playing with new toys, some just chasing each other. The grandparents looked enthusiastic, so happy to have these children in their lives.

Just like Hayley's grandparents would have been.

No.

Why did he keep doing that?

Any reference to a child, and he brought it back to Hayley. To what it was like to have a daughter.

In truth, he'd never had a daughter.

But could he? Someday?

Would it even be possible for April and him to go into such an experience without having grave reservations? Oscar imagined having a child who was completely normal – but always being on edge. Waiting for that child's entire life for them to burst into a large demon and try to maim everyone. He'd pay excessive attention to everything he did, making sure he was in control of his actions, worrying about the knife he'd use just to butter toast or cut up vegetables, and what some demonic influence the child may have would make him do with that knife.

Whatever happened, the niggling voice in the back of their head would always be there.

The parents of the children stood together in joyful discussion. The men held bottles of lager, as did a few of the women, though one of the women held a glass of wine. They kept making glances back to the children throughout their conversation, as if they were talking about them, constantly referring to their growth, or adorable habits, or life at school, or...

And there was Hazel.

Stood with them, but not really. She was there, but the conversation didn't involve her. She didn't have children. Or a spouse. She was alone, on the outside, looking in.

Oscar suddenly felt very close to her, despite only ever having one brief conversation.

He was tempted to go in just to make her feel better. To give her what she was lacking.

But then he decided.

He wasn't what she was lacking.

He never would be.

This was what life was like – family. Children. Grandparents. Meals. Socialising. Growing up, watching children grow up, talking about their school, their play habits, their friends.

This was the life Oscar dreamt of.

Strange. Before he'd discovered he was a Sensitive, he'd craved something more. He worked in a supermarket, never having the drive to do anything. He was hooked on anxiety medication. He did nothing but sit alone in his room, alternating between wallowing and masturbating. He craved to have a deeper purpose.

Now he had that deeper purpose, he craved that simple life.

This life, that these people had.

That's what he wanted with April, so much.

But, as he watched Hazel, watching her pained expression, he saw that he could never have it.

He wasn't like her.

And she wasn't like him.

She caught his gaze in hers.

He didn't hesitate. He turned and marched away, walking with as much pace as he could.

By the time Hazel had rushed out of the house to see whether she had seen what she thought she'd seen, he was gone, and she would never know whether he had actually been there.

Oscar stared blankly at Eddie.

With all those fears he'd used to get back to this room, the room in God-knows-where, he needed answers, and he needed them immediately.

"Where even are we?" Oscar asked.

"Where do you think we are?" Eddie responded, holding his arms out.

"Stop doing that. Stop answering my question with a question. Give me a straight answer."

"Does it frustrate you not to get a straight answer?"

"You are not a psychiatrist, so stop acting like one. Tell me what this place is."

Eddie looked around himself and took a smug breath inwards. Wherever it was, he acted like he owned it. Like it was somewhere he'd been many times before.

"Imagine somewhere real," he said, "and imagine somewhere not real. We're about in between."

"That doesn't make any sense."

"If there was a map with Heaven on one side, and Hell on the other – we'd be slap bang in the middle."

"So, like Purgatory?"

"If you need to put a name on it, then yes."

"How did I manage to get here so easily then?"

Eddie looked confused.

"Easily?"

"Yeah." Oscar stepped toward Eddie. He felt a confrontation brewing, and this time, he wasn't going to back down from it. "It seems like a tough place to get to."

"Well, evidently not, if you got here so easily."

"Quit doing that!"

"Doing what?"

Oscar's fists clenched. He sucked an angry breath of air and tried to stop his face from curling into a mockery of anger.

"Heaven and Hell and Purgatory, these are all places that take a lot of doing to get to, especially for someone who is not dead. All I had to do to get here was think about things I'm scared of. Seems strange."

"What's strange?"

"It's not even just the ease of it, Eddie. It's the method. How does thinking about fear take you to a place like this, if this is what you say it is?"

"You think I'm a liar?"

"I think things aren't that simple."

"Are they ever?"

"I said quit it!"

Oscar took another stride forward.

"Tell me the truth."

"I am."

"Tell me something about you. About your past."

"It doesn't matter who I am."

"Yes, it does."

Eddie went to speak but couldn't. His mouth was stuck, wide open. His eyes showed that this wasn't meant to happen.

He stuttered, stumbled, choking on his own lack of breath. He quivered, then seized.

Eddie tried to fight it, but he folded up like a cardboard box, and before Oscar's eyes could adjust, Eddie was gone.

Derek stood before him.

"Derek!" Oscar cried out, feeling a wave of relief, but unsure why.

"Oscar, you need to listen to me, because I don't have much time."

"What?"

"Last time I had seconds, I've managed to buy myself a little bit more."

"Why aren't you—"

"I'm not supposed to be here. I'm not allowed."

"Not allowed by who?"

Derek stepped forward. Placed a reassuring hand on Oscar's shoulder.

"It's about April," Derek stated.

"What? What about April?"

"She—" Derek choked. He couldn't talk. Something was in his throat, rising up.

He fell to his knees.

"Derek!" Oscar cried, going to his knees next to Derek.

Derek kept choking. And coughing. And choking and coughing and choking and coughing until he lurched, gagging, his whole body convulsing as he vomited. He spat out a thick worm, rings around its radius, dirty and large.

"Oscar... They are trying to stop me..."

"They? Who's they?"

"It's—"

He choked again.

Stuttered, just like Eddie had done.

"I'll find a way..." he whimpered.

Oscar stared. Listening. Hoping to hear more.

"I'll find a way to tell you..." Derek tried again, but before he could finish his sentence, he was gone.

And she was there.

And Oscar couldn't take it.

How could she be there?

If she wasn't dead, how could she be in this place?

"April?" Oscar asked.

She was on her knees. Her eyes weakly beseeching him, stuck between physical agony and mental torment. One arm reached out to him, the other covered her heart.

"April, what's going on?"

April took her hand away from her chest.

A gaping, open wound that would fit a knife perfectly glared back at him, blood trickling, then pouring, then covering them both in a pool beside their knees.

"April?"

"Oscar... my chest..."

She fell onto her back.

Her eyes emptied.

Oscar shook her. Put his hand on her cold cheek. Willed her to respond.

She did nothing.

"Apr–"

His eyes opened.

O'Neil stood before him with a flashlight. The room just as dark, just as cold, just as claustrophobic as it had ever been.

"What is going on?" Oscar said, quieter than he expected.

"What's that, lad?" O'Neil replied.

Oscar leapt to his feet and surged toward O'Neil, towering over him.

"What is going on!" Oscar demanded, this time louder.

"Did you see somethin' bad?" O'Neil asked.

Oscar didn't know what to say. He was torn between grabbing O'Neil by the scruff of his neck or falling to his knees and crying at O'Neil's feet.

"The place you went to was a place of fear," O'Neil said. "It's not a place for pleasant images. If you're disturbed, then it means you're finding your answers."

Oscar had no idea what to say. What to think. How to take it. His head pounded. His mind was drained, emptied of logic and replaced with manic, sporadic thoughts darting around like elusive words he couldn't reach.

"I–" Oscar went to speak, then realised he had no idea what he was going to say. "I just want to go to bed."

O'Neil nodded. "Right you are, lad."

Oscar followed O'Neil out, trying not to think, trying to make his mind numb.

21

No matter what Oscar did, what he thought of, what he willed himself to imagine – the image of April dying in his arms overpowered everything.

He'd seen it most nights. Her helpless face haunted his dreams. The same look of terror in her eyes as she realised she was going to die – that look could never leave him.

She'd press her hands over her heart and look at Oscar with wounded eyes, crying out to him again and again, "My chest... Oscar, my chest..."

But this was worse.

In dreams, they were just images. Obscure photographs placed in a random order. There was nothing he could smell, nothing he could touch – just the look on her face.

This time, he'd held her in his arms. He'd run his hand down her cheek. He'd felt the desperate sweat that marked her soft skin.

He'd even tasted her scent. Her natural, comforting aroma mixed with delicate doses of perfume.

That's what made him think it was her.

That it was real.

How would someone fake her smell?

How would an image produce such a thing?

But these weren't the most prominent questions troubling him. The most important, most crucial, most dominant question was the one he dreaded to answer:

Is she still alive?

After all, wherever it was he had gone to, he'd only been able to see people who were dead.

He picked up his phone.

What now?

Just give her a call and ask her if she's alive?

After all this?

"Hey, sorry for leaving you heartbroken and not speaking to you, but I just wanted to check, are you alive?"

No.

He couldn't talk to her. Not like this. This wasn't the way he'd pictured their reunion.

But he still had to hear her voice.

Had to know. Had to have some indication.

But then again, what if the image he saw was a premonition, rather than her current state?

Stop overthinking.

Disregarding all further worries, he found April's number in his phone.

His thumb lingered over it. Poised.

He called her.

Placing the phone firmly against his ear, he waited. Sat on the edge of the bed, wondering why it was ringing for so long.

Then she answered.

"Hello?"

It was her. Her voice. She was alive. She was there. It was all nonsense; none of it was true, none of it.

"Hello?" she repeated.

What if he spoke to her?

Just opened his mouth, let his voice carry out words, let her know he was okay. Let her know how much he missed her.

Screw it.

I'm going to do it. I'm going to talk to her.

"Hello? Is anyone there?"

He went to talk, full of energy, ready for this, sure of his decision, then–

Nothing.

No words came out.

No sentences formed.

He couldn't. He couldn't say anything.

"Oscar?" April said.

Oscar tensed. His breath caught in his throat.

"Oscar, is that you?"

He willed tears away. Willed himself to have strength. To not put this burden on her. To find out answers before he re-entered her life.

"Oscar, if that is you, it's okay."

No, April.

It's not okay.

You don't know.

Nothing is okay.

"Oscar, please – please come home."

Oscar closed his eyes. Listened to that voice. Oh, how much he missed that voice.

"Oscar, come home. I miss you."

Oh, I miss you too. Miss you more than anything. I need you. Please, just...

He hung up.

Dangled the phone loosely before letting it drop, thudding on the broken floorboards.

She missed him.

That's what she'd said.

"I miss you, too," he said.

"Where are you?" she would have said.

"In Edinburgh," he'd have said.

"If you leave now, you could be here by morning."

"I could."

"I love you."

"I love you so much."

But he didn't say that.

He didn't say a single word of it.

He just said nothing.

22

THE WHIRRING TONE OF A DEAD PHONE LINE REPEATED THROUGH the speaker on April's phone.

She kept it to her ear, hoping it wasn't real, it was just her mind playing tricks on her. That he hadn't hung up. That he'd spoken to her.

If that was him.

Who else could it have been?

For all she knew, Oscar could be dead. Killed by a demon. Killed by himself. Killed by drink and drugs that wouldn't flush out his thoughts.

She wished he hadn't left.

She played the scene out in the theatre of her mind any time she let it wander. The two weeks it took for him to come home, and that's what she thought he was doing – coming home. But he wasn't. He was just coming to say goodbye.

Was he coming back?

He hadn't said, but she'd always assumed. Thought that he would.

She looked around their bedroom.

She'd kept it just as he left it.

Photos of their happiness pinned to the wall by nails. Images of what was and what could be decorating the walls of her solace. They had arms around each other, they were smiling, they were laughing, they were joking, they were posing. They were doing everything but what they were doing now.

That's how it should be.

She left the bedroom. Walked down the stairs, passing more pictures hanging firmly on the wall.

Her phone beeped.

Her heart leapt. Could that be him? A text message apologising for not saying anything? Reassuring her that he'd be home soon?

She looked at her phone.

Julian.

It was Julian.

Not that she wasn't grateful to hear from him, but it wasn't what she was hoping for.

She opened the text message.

No luck. Still can't track him down. I'll keep searching.

Just what she was expecting Julian to say.

She'd never asked Julian to try to find Oscar, mind. She'd never asked it. But he'd done it.

She thought that Julian felt partly responsible somehow, but wasn't sure why. The only one who should feel responsible was the demon that had occupied her womb, then her–

What's done is done.

And cannot be undone.

So quit picking it apart.

She was sure Julian was searching for himself, too. Or for Oscar, however unlikely that may be. They hadn't always been the best of friends. Maybe Julian felt that the journey Oscar had set off on was futile. Was unneeded. That Oscar didn't have to go running away for answers, and that Julian could have helped more in that respect.

Julian had offered to go abroad to find Oscar, but April had begged him not to. The last thing she needed was for Julian to go too. If he did, then she would truly be alone.

He had taken her off the streets as a teenager and introduced her to her gift. He was the closest thing she had to an older brother, or even a father figure.

She couldn't have him abandon her too.

She put the kettle on. Watched the water lay still, then simmer, then boil. Without consciously telling herself too, she made a coffee and took it into the living room.

She put the television on. Curled up on the sofa. Clasped the coffee in both hands. Pulled the blanket over her.

What she'd give to have Oscar next to her.

She wasn't even confident doing her job without him. It was her responsibility to channel the spirits – that was her gift for being a Sensitive. She was able to take spirits or demons or the dead and allow them into her body to talk through her.

But there always had to be someone there to make sure that whatever spoke through her, left. That it chose not to stay. That, while Julian was doing whatever he needed to do, the prayers were recited.

Oscar had stumbled once, when he first started. Since then, he had never let her down. Without fail he had perfectly exorcised whatever entity was using her as a conduit and done it within seconds.

What if that entity didn't leave now?

What if she let one in unknowingly – as she'd done by accident a few times before she'd learnt about what she was – and then it wouldn't leave? What if she opened herself up without realising, and one of them chose to stay in her?

She would lose herself completely.

Just as she'd done when she'd had the demon inside her womb. The thing that came out, that Oscar called Hayley, that had called him Daddy. That had called her Mummy.

That had controlled Oscar and manipulated him into trying to kill her.

That wasn't him. She knew that. He knew that.

Except, did he?

He couldn't have.

Because he left.

He left.

He left.

He left.

Over and over the words repeated.

He left.

He left.

He left he left he left he left he left he left he left he left.

And now she was vulnerable.

And now she was alone.

THEN

23

O'Neil wasn't, nor had he ever been, the affectionate type.

Sometimes he reasoned with himself that this was because he'd never had someone to be affectionate toward. Being a priest meant a vow of celibacy, so that meant he never had a wife or a family to be close to; and the one indiscretion he'd had led to a daughter that didn't want to know him.

He wasn't close to his parents. His mother had died when he was a child, and his father would rather have shown O'Neil the harsh side of his belt than a hug. He'd had an older sister, but she had moved to America by the time he was an adult, meaning he had little to no contact with her, except for the occasional birthday message or Christmas card.

So, sitting by the side of Father Elijah Harris's bed, holding his mentor's hand, had taken a lot for him to do. Yet, at the same time, it had been effortless; not even a decision. Harris had been ill for a while. Cancer, they had said, and now he was in the early stages of recovery.

O'Neil didn't blame cancer for Harris's condition.

He had no doubt such a thing was involved, but Harris had

taught him better than that. He didn't accept such things as given, and he unequivocally believed that, should Harris never have put himself in harm's way, such an illness would never have found him.

Harris had always taught O'Neil: *being an exorcist makes you vulnerable.* O'Neil had never believed it until he'd had to watch the one man he looked up to, and his only friend in the world, suffer in the way he had.

"They say you're on track," O'Neil said. "They say you're showing signs of beating this."

"Then why do I feel like shit?" Harris asked.

Most people would have taken this as an abrasive retort. O'Neil knew Harris well enough to know it was humour. Blatant, on-the-nose, no-qualms-about-it humour.

O'Neil even allowed himself a guilty chuckle.

"It can't be easy. They've had to do a lot to you."

"Tell me about it," Harris said. "The sons of bitches. And here I thought it was my time to go. I was actually looking forward to it, and they had to go and bugger it all up."

O'Neil allowed himself another chuckle. Odd, really, how this was the man who had shouted at O'Neil, berated him, picked him apart and tore him down.

At the end of it, O'Neil had become a better exorcist, and a better man.

So he couldn't complain.

"I've prepared a spare room for you," O'Neil told Harris. "So I can keep an eye on you. So that I can make sure everything is okay."

"That's kind of you, but not necessary."

"I know your ego won't like it, but I don't care. I'm helping."

Harris turned his head slowly toward O'Neil, his droopy eyes smiling at him.

"Thank you. You are a good friend."

"I like to think you'd do the same with me."

"You kidding? The minute I can be rid of you, I'm dumping you with the fishes. They can have you."

O'Neil smiled again.

"I'll leave you to sleep."

"Yes, I–"

Harris grew pale, as if a tub of paint had just spread down his face. He stiffened like a board, his eyes abruptly wide with terror, wider than they could have been in this sleep state.

"What?" O'Neil said, looking around himself, trying to see what Harris was staring at. "What is it?"

"Connor," Harris spoke, his voice shivering, weak. "Connor, you–"

A nurse walked in.

"Come on now, Father Harris, it's time for you to sleep," she said, lifting his pillow and raising her eyebrows at O'Neil in a way that told him it was time to go.

Harris didn't take his eyes away.

"What is it? Tell me, what is it?"

Harris didn't speak. His mouth stayed open, but nothing but broken breaths pushed out.

"Time to go, Father," the nurse instructed him.

O'Neil backed away, not letting go of Harris's tormented eyes. Harris was fixed rigidly, terror written upon him, and O'Neil could do nothing but leave.

He ran through the corridor, bumping into a nurse, and into the men's toilets. He found himself halting next to a mirror and peering at his reflection, looking himself in the eyes, his face, around himself, up and down, upon his robes, upon his hands.

There was nothing.

Absolutely nothing.

Nothing at all that was–

Light flickered on his hands.

He looked to the roof.

The lights overhead, each of them in perfect unison, flickered, spraying light with an impulsive glimmer.

He looked at his reflection.

With every flash of darkness, he saw something. He couldn't see what it was. But it was there. Distorted features, contorted expression.

He pushed his face closer to the mirror, closer, closer, until his nose was pressed against it.

His eyes turned red, then turned back.

In his eyes, he saw something else.

He couldn't breathe. He couldn't move. He couldn't even scream.

Being an exorcist makes you vulnerable.

Harris's wise words rang true.

O'Neil knew it better than anyone now.

He knew it conclusively.

Because, as he searched his eyes, searching his face, he recognised the unmistakable truth.

He was not alone.

NOW

24

By choosing the same bench, Oscar felt it was inevitable that he would run into Hazel, and maybe he intended it that way. It was his subconscious that had led him there, but his deliberate decision that had made him take a seat and sip on his coffee to go.

It didn't take long before the familiar face appeared at his side.

"Well," Hazel said jokingly, "come here to explain why you stood me up?"

"I'm sorry." Oscar forced a sympathetic smile. "I just couldn't make it."

"Excuses!"

"No, honestly. Why would I stand you up? You're probably the closest thing I actually have to a friend in this city."

That seemed to perk her up.

"Hey, I'm on my lunch hour, would you like some company?" she asked. "You can totally say no, I would not be offended. Like, I wouldn't want some weirdo who invited me to some meal with their family without even knowing you to sit and have–"

"I would love some company. Please sit."

"I'll be right back," she said with a large smile, and hurried away.

Oscar had barely taken a few sips before she reappeared, this time with a coffee of her own.

She sat beside him and perched on the edge of her seat. She really was pretty. Though very different to April. One thing Oscar loved about April was her kookiness – the way she dyed her hair purple, wore baggy jeans, wore women's boxers. Everything about April made her different to everyone else. With Hazel, she was gorgeous, but in the same way that every other gorgeous woman in the world was gorgeous.

"So how long you here for?" she asked.

"Where? The bench?"

"In Edinburgh, silly."

"Oh. Right." He considered the question. He hadn't really set a length of time to be there. He was pretty much planning on staying as long as it took. "I guess indefinitely."

"Indefinitely? You may as well just move here. It's a great place to live."

"Have you lived here long?"

"I did my undergrad at the uni. Now I'm looking at doing my master's. Just kicking about in this job while I figure it all out."

"What are you looking to do a master's in?"

She hid behind a playful smile. "You don't want to know."

"Of course I do. Tell me."

"You'll laugh."

"I promise I won't."

"Fine." She shifted position, getting comfortable, circling her coffee with her stirrer. "It's in drama and performance."

Oscar stuck his bottom lip out.

"Was not expecting that."

"You think it's silly?"

"No, of course not. You like to act then? Been in much?"

"Mainly just amateur dramatics stuff. Like, local theatres, performances with friends. I plan to do the fringe festival next year."

"What's that?"

"What's the fringe festival? Like, the biggest arts festival in the world. What Edinburgh is known for. You honestly never heard of it?"

"Can't say that I have."

"You should really look into the place you're going to before you get there."

Something occurred to Oscar. Something a little strange. "How did you know I don't live here?"

She shrugged her shoulders nonchalantly.

"Could just tell. So what do you do for a job?"

What does he do for a job?

Where would he even start?

How much would she even believe?

"I…" he said, deliberating between honesty and evasion. "I guess I'm in between things at the moment."

"Okay, so what are you in between?"

Oscar decided not to answer. To let the question linger between them so that it could wilt and fade.

"You should know," Oscar said, "I have a girlfriend."

"That's fine."

"You sure?"

"Don't assume every girl who talks to you is hitting on you, Oscar. Maybe some of us are just as desperate for company as you."

Hazel frowned. Like something was hurting her.

"What's wrong?"

Hazel grabbed her chest.

"What is it?"

Her eyes reached out weakly to Oscar.

"Hazel, what is it?"

"My chest, it hurts."

"What is it that–"

Wait.

Hang on.

Something felt oddly familiar.

"My chest," Hazel said again, placing both hands over her heart.

No.

No, no, no.

What is going on?

What is going on?

"My chest... Oscar, my chest..."

Oscar stood.

"Who are you?" Oscar asked.

"My chest!"

People turned to look.

She punched her fist against the bench, jarring her coffee into a puddle on the floor.

Oscar just stared. Poised between staying and going. Poised between confusion and perplexity.

"Oscar, help me!"

"What – what do you want me to do?"

"Just help me! It's fine, it's hardly like I'm going to run and tell April!"

Oscar couldn't move.

The hairs on his arms stood on end.

His entire body tensed.

His heart beat against his ribs like it was trying to destroy them.

"Hazel, I never told you my girlfriend's name was April."

She looked to him, distressed, sweaty, disgruntled, her hair hanging over her face, fist still clinging to her chest.

"Get out my way if you're not going to help," she snapped, and charged past Oscar toward a nearby public bathroom.

He watched her go, then grabbed his jacket and left.

He swore – he absolutely swore – he had never told Hazel April's name.

But she had known.

Somehow, she had known.

25

BY THE TIME HE ARRIVED BACK TO O'NEIL'S, OSCAR HAD ALMOST ridden the incident in the coffee shop from his mind.

If he replayed the scene again, just to see if he did actually mention April's name, he would probably go crazy – if he hadn't already.

Was there any other way Hazel could have known? Was there something he'd said the other day, something written down, any other way that Hazel could have picked up on April's name?

He decided he had to stop thinking about it.

It was needlessly panicking him. It could be nothing.

But that's not what his gut told him.

He knocked on O'Neil's door, waiting for an answer. Waiting for that grumpy face to swing it ajar, bark something unnecessarily nasty at him, and let him in.

O'Neil didn't.

He knocked again.

Nothing.

He tried the door. Oddly enough, it was unlocked. Oscar

couldn't remember whether or not O'Neil kept his door unlocked, but it was another thing that put him on edge.

He entered the living room, coated in darkness, and that's where he found O'Neil. Sat in an armchair, his head leant back over the head rest, his mouth wide open, snoring incessantly. It was an unattractive image, but a reassuring one. Nothing had happened. He was just asleep.

Oscar decided he'd try to do the same.

He removed his jacket, hung it by the door, and began his ascent up the stairs, trudging on every step, dreading how hard he was probably going to find it to get to sleep. Wondering if he should try phoning April again, maybe actually speak to her this time; but then again, what would be the point? What would he say? That he's not coming back? That he knows nothing new?

No, he'd just close his eyes and hope for the best.

He opened the bathroom door, the creak of which coincided with another sound. Faintly, coming from downstairs, Oscar was sure he heard a bell ringing.

He paused, waiting. Listening intently. Seeing if he heard it once more.

Silence.

Discomforting, reassuring, silence.

He entered the bathroom.

Ding-a-ling.

His body stiffened.

He was sure he heard it this time.

That's when he remembered – the bell downstairs. The one that O'Neil used to use when he lived with other exorcists. The bell they would ring as a warning to the rest of the house – something was here.

Oscar crept into the bedroom and took his crucifix from his bag. Squeezing it tightly, he edged along the corridor and paused at the top of the stairs.

Ding-a-ling.

Was O'Neil signalling to him?

Was he in need of help?

Oscar tiptoed down the steps, eager to avoid the creaks they inevitably brought in their old age. He reached the final step and peered around the door, peering into the same darkness that had encompassed the room when he'd arrived back minutes ago.

He pushed his head slowly into the room.

O'Neil hadn't moved.

He remained motionless, snoring away, an unpleasant image of a tired, bitter old man.

The bell remained on the fireplace, untouched.

Nothing else was in the room. Nothing.

O'Neil couldn't have rung it.

Surely.

He was asleep.

Oscar decided he was hearing things, probably his paranoia – the mind invented hallucinations sometimes, especially when it was tired, or anxious. And boy, was he tired and anxious.

He allowed his breathing to calm, and he turned back to the stairs.

He'd barely placed his foot on the next step before he heard it again.

This time, it rang more than once.

Ding-a-ling. Ding-a-ling. Ding-a-ling.

He paced back into the room, crucifix ready, marching toward the bell.

He looked from the bell to O'Neil. Still snoring. Back to the bell, to O'Neil. The bell. O'Neil.

He lifted the bell.

There, inside of it, was a note.

He glanced once more to O'Neil. Fast asleep. Completely unaware.

Oscar removed the note.

He unfolded it. Just five simple words:

Do not trust Father O'Neil.

He stared at the note.

Stared.

Clueless how to react.

"What the hell are you doing with my bell!" snapped O'Neil, standing up and wide awake.

26

Oscar scrunched the note and shoved it in his pocket, staring at O'Neil so O'Neil's eyes would meet his and be diverted from the secret buried within his fist, his fist he was casually placing in his pocket.

"What?" Oscar said, startled.

"I said, what the hell are you doing with my bell? I told you not to touch it!"

Oscar looked to the bell nestled in his hand and back to O'Neil.

"I – I – I –"

"You what, lad? What? Sometime before I die, yeah?"

"I – I was just – I thought I heard it ringing. I thought I heard it."

O'Neil's eyes drifted south, to the arm stuffed into Oscar's trousers.

"What have you got there?"

"Got where?" Oscar answered, a little too quickly.

"In your hand?"

"Nothing," Oscar said, withdrawing his hand and opening

his fist wide, waving his hand around, doing everything to prove that there was nothing there.

"You put it in your pocket. What is it? What have you stolen?"

"Nothing, Father. There is nothing in my pocket. I haven't stolen anything."

O'Neil leered at Oscar. Wondering. Trying to suss him out.

"I promise you," Oscar said. "I have stolen nothing. I was just looking at the bell."

"Well put it down," O'Neil demanded. "I told you not to play with it. Don't you listen? Or are you too busy just tryin' a have a craic at an old man's expense?"

"I swear, I am not trying to do anything to disrespect you."

O'Neil took a step closer. So close Oscar could smell the ageing garlic in the old man's breath.

"Come on," O'Neil decided. "We're going out."

"Where to?"

"To put you in another trance. It's time I had leave of you, and the sooner we can get your answer, the quicker you can be gone."

"Honestly, I think I should just go to bed–"

"I don't care what you think, you little gobshite! You're in my house, breaking my rules, and I'm thinking I want you gone. So get your coat."

Oscar cautiously edged himself toward the front door, to where he had hung his coat. O'Neil followed, then patted his pockets and cursed under his breath.

"Ah, darn it, my keys."

O'Neil turned and waddled through the living room, toward the kitchen, where his keys were kept.

Oscar felt for the slip of paper in his pocket.

It wasn't there.

The slip of paper wasn't there.

He searched his other pocket. The pockets of his jacket, even though he knew he'd only just put it on.

Not there.

His eyes searched the floor, and that's when he saw it.

On the living room floor.

In O'Neil's path.

"What's this!" O'Neil grumbled.

Oscar put his hand on the door handle, ready to run.

O'Neil grabbed the piece of paper, screwed up into a ball, secured in the palm of his hand.

"Leavin' your rubbish in my house…" O'Neil muttered, making his way to the kitchen.

When O'Neil entered the kitchen, he closed the door.

Oscar realised he was still clutching the crucifix.

He put it in his inside jacket pocket.

And he waited.

Watched the kitchen door. Watched it. Shut. Mumbles behind it. Shuffles behind it.

Had O'Neil read it?

Seconds later the door reopened, and O'Neil simply stood there, silent. Staring at Oscar. Glaring, more like.

Both of them watched the other, in a standoff, neither flinching, neither moving.

But Oscar could feel his heart thudding. He tried to conceal the speed of his breath, but he knew his eyes were wide, and he was just waiting, waiting for the moment, waiting for something to happen.

"Well?" O'Neil finally said. "Shall we go then?"

Oscar realised he was stood in front of the door, still holding the door handle.

He opened the door.

Stepped out.

O'Neil followed, locking the door behind him.

O'Neil stopped outside the door. Looked at Oscar once

more. Sharing another contest of willpower, another moment of mutual eye contact, both of them thinking very different things.

"This way," O'Neil said, and walked on.

Oscar followed, patting his crucifix, checking it was still there.

As if it would save him.

As if it would make a single bit of difference.

27

THROUGH THE SAME CHURCH, BETWEEN THE SAME PEWS, TOWARD the same altar.

Except this time, Oscar felt like he was marching to his funeral. Like he was carrying his own casket.

The whole walk felt like an omen of death. A grave, sinister undercurrent to every step.

Neither he nor O'Neil had said a single word during the journey. Neither of them had broken the turgid silence. O'Neil had walked like he always did, led Oscar the same route they had three times already – and the entire time, Oscar was just watching, waiting for something. Anything. Some change in O'Neil's demeanour, an act of aggression, of anger, some evidence that there was something there for him to fear.

But there wasn't.

Just a feeling.

And a note now discarded.

O'Neil lifted the grate that led to the underground corridor and, ultimately, to the room where Oscar's trance states had been so far.

Oscar had no intention of going into another trance.

But he had to play this out. He had to wait. Had to be sensible. He wasn't sure of anything, and that was the one thing he was sure of – and, until he knew what to do, how to act, he had to act like he always had.

"After you," O'Neil said.

Oscar climbed down.

O'Neil followed, closing the grate behind them.

O'Neil withdrew his flashlight and led them to the small room, the walls of which seemed to have closed further in, though Oscar knew that they hadn't.

"Well?" O'Neil prompted. "Are you ready?"

Then O'Neil smiled. Something Oscar hadn't seen before. But something about that smile was different. It was unlike the face he'd seen before.

There was something deeply disturbing about that smile.

Something undeniably sinister.

THEN

O'NEIL, FOR THE FIRST TIME IN HIS LIFE, UNDERSTOOD WHY HIS daughter had resented him the way he did.

He'd allowed the demon into her life, and she had suffered.

Suffered like he was suffering now.

It felt like a hundred claws digging into his head, squirming about his mind and removing any memory, thought, or feeling remotely associated with happiness.

It was removing anything about this place on this Earth.

He was in there, somewhere. He knew he was. But he was in the backseat, and he couldn't see who was driving. He could just see the back of their head. And it was something far more evil than he'd allowed himself to believe.

This was, after all, the first time he'd ever actually seen one of these demons in its truest form. And that was because, this time, it was inside of him.

"Holy Lord, heavenly Father," commanded the strong words of Father Elijah Harris, his presence taking the whole room.

Harris had sworn he'd never do this again. That he was done. After recovering from his illness, he just didn't have the strength, or the energy.

Then this happened. He received word of what he had always feared.

Father Connor O'Neil was suffering from demonic possession.

Nothing else would have compelled him to exit his retirement with as much vigour and determination as this.

"Our Lord Jesus Christ, who once and for all consigned that fallen and apostate tyrant to the flames of Hell, sent as Your son to crush that roaring lion, hasten to our call!"

O'Neil was unrecognisable. In a padded room, his arms held to the wall by chains, the rest of his body moaned and groaned and curled and entwined. On every line of prayer, O'Neil's body would rise into the air of its own accord, lifting his legs above his head, rising away from the restraints that were the only thing keeping O'Neil's body down.

"Strike terror, Lord, into the beast now laying waste in your vineyard!"

O'Neil's face was different. Worse than Harris had ever seen.

The face of the possessed was always pale, always wounded, the pupils always fully dilated.

O'Neil's face wasn't just pale, it was falling off in rags.

It wasn't wounded, it was ripped to shreds.

His pupils weren't just fully dilated – they consumed his entire eyeball with black and red.

His teeth had curved. This wasn't just a demon taking control, this was a demon taking over. O'Neil wasn't being attacked like other possessed victims, he was being removed. More and more his body was taking the form of the demon surging through him, and more and more, O'Neil's personality was seeping away.

"Fill your servants with courage to fight manfully against that reprobate dragon, lest he despise those who put trust in you, and say of Pharaoh of old – I know not God, nor will I set Israel free."

"Your God did nothing…" came voices that no human vocal cord could produce, neither independently, nor simultaneously. "He won't listen to you now…"

"Let your mighty hand cast him out of Your servant, Father Connor O'Neil, so he may no longer hold captive this person whom it please You in Your image, and whom You redeemed through Your son."

"Because it's helpless… *you* are helpless…"

Harris wiped the perspiration from his forehead. Sweat was trickling into his eyes, but he couldn't give up.

Even though he knew, by now, it was beyond hope.

"Repeat my command!" Harris demanded of the priest stood behind him, cowering, pathetic, childish – the priest who was reluctantly made to assist because no one else would. "I command you, unclean spirit!"

"I command you, unclean spirit," echoed the wobbling voice of the assisting priest.

"Louder, dammit! I command you, unclean spirit!"

"I command you, unclean spirit!"

Harris held his crucifix out, held it tightly.

"Along with your minion attacking this servant of God!"

"Along with your minion attacking this servant of God!"

"Free your child! Free him from this demon's shackles!"

"Free your child! Free him from this demon's shackles!"

The demon roared with laughter.

"As you wish…"

The demon ripped the restraints from the wall and rose into the air.

Harris dropped his *Rites of Exorcism.*

Dropped his crucifix.

Dropped to his knees.

He'd known it, but now it became sorely apparent.

He was too late.

He was much too late.

NOW

29

O'Neil looked to Oscar expectantly. But this wasn't just an old man's impatience, this was different – it wasn't someone waiting for Oscar, it was some*thing* waiting for the final curtain.

"You know what to do," O'Neil said. "Are you not going to start?"

"No," Oscar answered.

"I beg your pardon?"

"No, I am not," Oscar responded defiantly.

O'Neil laughed, a deep, croaky laugh, a laugh that was not his own.

"You fool."

Oscar backed away.

O'Neil shook his head. Grinning lecherously. Laughing irately.

"I will not," Oscar insisted. "I will not do it. I will not go there again."

"You think you're the one who put you there?"

"What?"

O'Neil stepped toward Oscar, but Oscar continued circling, staying to the wall farthest away from O'Neil.

"Trying to get you to think of all your fears worked for me, it helped make me stronger – but did you ever really think it was just a trance you were in? That you *chose* to be in it? Honestly, did you ever really think it was up to you?"

"What?"

"And did you ever really think you chose when to come back?"

"No, you're lying."

"I could send you there and trap you there and you would have no choice."

"I don't believe you."

O'Neil raised his hands.

"Back away!" Oscar demanded.

"A te, de l'essere, principo immenso, materio e spirito, ragione e senso," O'Neil chanted in a low hum.

"What are you doing?"

"Te invoco, o Satana, re del convito."

Oscar fell to his knees.

How was this happening?

"You can't do this," Oscar declared. "I'm a Sensitive, I can fight you."

O'Neil guffawed, practically falling over his laughter, almost to his knees.

"You really think so?" O'Neil said, but something had changed. His Irish accent had gone. He was speaking in another accent… Like a hybrid of various other accents…

Oscar shook his head.

He closed his eyes. Willed himself to resist whatever O'Neil was trying to do.

Come on, he told himself. *You are stronger than this. You can't let him do anything to you.*

"Have you not learnt all about being a Sensitive yet?" O'Neil taunted. "About how it actually, really, when it all comes down to it, means nothing?"

Oscar concentrated, he didn't know what on, but he concentrated nonetheless, not on his fears this time, but on his strength, as hard as it was to find.

He thought of April.

Thought of her, not in fear, but to give him willpower, to give him–

"There's no point thinking about her now."

Oscar's eyes shot wide open.

"No, I can't read your mind. But I can smell your fear. She's all over you."

Oscar shook his head. This was a test. It was something trying him. Trying to undo his resolve. He couldn't let it win.

April could be his strength, not his weakness.

"She's next," O'Neil said.

Oscar looked to O'Neil with horror.

April was next?

A shot rang through his body. He seized, closed his eyes to stand the pain, then he was gone.

When he opened them again, O'Neil was no longer there.

He was back in the plain room.

The Between.

And there was no exit in sight.

THEN

30

"I'm sorry, Connor," gasped Harris. "Really, I am."

The demon rose into the air, spreading its claws, filling O'Neil's body.

"Father Connor O'Neil's not here right now."

Harris shook his head. Fell to his knees.

Not in denial, but in confirmation.

He knew O'Neil was gone.

Gone from this world.

He had been away from O'Neil for too long. Enjoying a happy retirement, something very few exorcists were ever afforded. He never knew what was happening in his absence.

And how long it had been happening for.

"So," Harris said, striking a reluctant conversation with the demon. "How long?"

O'Neil's expression turned to that of perplexity.

"I mean, how long have you been there? How long did it take for you to do it?"

"Oh, not long," the demon replied, a sinister arrogance in its voice. "A year, give or take."

Harris nodded.

He'd seen it before.

Amalgamation incarnation.

Even if you ridded the body of the demon, all you would be left with now would be a body. O'Neil's place had been taken.

O'Neil was somewhere else now, likely suffering an eternity of damnation and torture.

"Just do it," Harris said, bowing his head, helplessly sobbing, the last grip he had on an honourable death leaving with his tears.

"Oh, no," the demon replied. "I'm going to relish this."

"Just… Please… Do it…"

"You have been the scourge of Hell. You have fought so many of us, you have defeated so many of us… and now, look at us. Together like two old friends. And you think I'm not going to relish it?"

Harris lifted his head, his cheeks smudged, his face despondent.

"Please, have mercy."

"Mercy!"

The demon roared, sending the priest left to assist against the far wall, rendering him unconscious.

Harris remained on his knees.

Right where the demon wanted him.

"At least tell me your name," Harris pleaded. "At least tell me who it is I have finally lost to."

"My name is Agramon," the demon replied, full of cockiness, freely gloating.

"Agramon…" Harris confirmed. He knew the demon well. "The demon of fear…"

The demon descended, landing its knees gently before Harris, until they were both kneeling, looking into each other's eyes, inches away from each other's face.

Harris could smell the demon's stink. Like rotting flesh, or mouldy remains of discarded meat. It burnt.

He knew he should try to kill it, but his body wasn't what it once was. Retirement had allowed him to grow weak and feeble. And, even if he could put up a fight against this kind of power, he didn't know whether he could kill something that was once his eldest friend.

No, there was no use. He'd defeated a great many demons in his time. What was one loss to add to a gleaming record?

"Are you not going to fight?" the demon asked.

"No," Harris replied. "There is no need."

"There is no need?"

"You have won. There is no way to defeat a demon who has taken the place of one of God's servants on this Earth. I am ready and willing to meet my death."

O'Neil grinned.

Agramon grinned.

"Ah, well," he said. "Best not to disappoint."

With a quick flash of a nail, Harris's throat bore a thin slit across its width.

Harris didn't struggle, didn't fight it. He allowed the pain to shock him, allowed his throat to grow warm with the trickle of his blood. Allowed his breath to cease, as he waited for the end.

At least, unlike O'Neil, he knew his passage to Heaven would be clear.

In his final moments, he said a prayer for his friend.

Not aloud, but in his mind.

Wishing that God would have mercy. That God would reach into Hell and pull him out.

But he knew that God wouldn't.

God didn't do that kind of thing.

Hell was the devil's domain.

With a final look into the demon's eyes, that leer that held such glee, such immense pleasure, he tried to see the face of his old friend. Tried searching for those eyes in there somewhere

That face was gone. Those eyes would never return.

He fell onto his front. Blood trickled into a pool, which expanded, then ended.

Harris' final second of suffocation ceased.

Agramon smiled.

His revenge was complete.

And no one knew who really filled this body but him.

His next targets were the Sensitives.

He would pick them off one by one. Drive them insane from their fear so they would drive themselves to death.

And he would start with the weakest.

NOW

THE WAITING HAD BEEN WORTH IT.

The days wallowing alone in the house. Never doing what he stole this skin to do.

Because human skin is vile. You should know that.

It tastes 'off.' It stretches so weakly, it's as if it could break at any moment – and often, it does. A simple scratch, and blood would announce itself like an unwelcome friend bursting through the door.

Sunshine hurt those fragile eyes. Those weak excuses for vision.

And other people. They were the worst thing about it.Looking at you like they are your equal. Like they have something in common, like they deserve to share this world with you, like their life has meaning or consequence or point.

So why bother?

If this encasing is such a disgusting mess, then why steal it? Why put yourself inside of it and take it from the pathetic human whose soul originally dwelled within?

Because of the opportunity.

There are limited ways for a demon to enter Earth.

Impregnating the spawn of a human. A perilously tiresome act to commit, and one that often has such little payoff – you are stuck as a child for so long, forcing your actions to be committed through a father until you are finally formed.

There are rituals. For those, however, you must command humans to commit such a ritual, which often involves possession in itself – but possession for another demon's gain.

Unless it was for the devil himself, why bother? Why relinquish a place on this Earth to another demon? You want it for your own.

Yes, the most feasible way to enter this world is to latch onto a human being's soul and take over their body until you have taken their place on this Earth.

Then it's like a free-for-all. A buffet of disasters. For the little time this body lasts, you have access to all mankind, to do what you will, what you need.

Agramon, the strongest fear demon the pits of Hell had to offer, had been elated when he'd had the opportunity. Not just to cause Father Connor O'Neil the pain he deserved, not just to kill Father Elijah Harris with the hand of one of the few that bastard cared about – but because fear is something all humans share.

They stink of it.

Every one of them has something – normally multiple somethings – that he could latch onto. Increase. Play-on. Use to drive that soul insane, until they were a wreck of the person they once claimed to be.

That's when his fatal claw would swoop down and the true form would be revealed, and that person's life would be ceased in inscrutable suffering.

Oscar had proven difficult. Being a Sensitive, he could almost pick up on those times his fear had been played on. The fear was easy to prick in him, but the death was hard to come-by.

Suppose being a Sensitive does have an advantage, even if Agramon – sorry, *O'Neil* – never allowed Oscar to learn it. Killing Oscar would have been a long, drawn-out, tough, strenuous process. The solution? Trap Oscar somewhere he would be left to die of his own accord. There was no way to escape from The Between that O'Neil had found – it was not on this world, nor in any supernatural realm. It was caught between Heaven and Hell, but far away from Purgatory. It was somewhere only the dead could access.

But somewhere O'Neil had still been able to manipulate.

He called himself O'Neil because that's the image he had to portray.

But he'd had to be restful. Patient. Wait in this mortal prison in that invalid's house, keeping the sunlight shut out, waiting.

Ever since he had been contacted by the Vatican.

Told that someone was coming for answers.

Asked if he could be of assistance.

To a Sensitive.

The scourge of the underworld. The enemy of Hell. The only defence between them and a full-on annihilation, a mass possession. The three that stood in the way

There were more Sensitives, of course. But most of them don't seem to know what they are. They go about their business, thinking the things they see out of the corner of their eye are just their imagination. There were just three that played on their gifts.

Gifts.

They treated it like a curse. They took what they had and claimed it was a burden.

Now the one that seemed to tie them all together had been incapacitated.

Two were left.

If the first was that easy, the next two would be quick.

It was the same method. Fear, madness, death. A quick succession of downfalls.

And man had many downfalls.

O'Neil sat on a train. A child smiled at him.

He grinned back.

He imagined peeling that child's skin from his face and licking his skull dry.

Imagined sticking his claw in that child's gut and tearing him apart from the inside.

Imagined entwining his claws into that child's mouth into the oesophagus until his lungs were ripped his heart was burst his eyes had cried and he was moaning in pain begging for his mother who was already laying dead beside his feet as he bled and bled and bled and bled and bled and bled and bled.

"Hi," the kid said.

"Fuck off," O'Neil subtly replied.

The child winced away and cuddled up to its oblivious mother.

O'Neil looked out the window at this wretched world.

Mass possession.

Hell's backdoor.

An apocalyptic vision.

Two more to dispatch that stood in his way.

He was on a one-way trip to Gloucestershire.

The devil will be so proud.

3 2

OSCAR FELT LIKE HIS BRAIN WAS POUNDING AGAINST HIS SKULL.

Which was difficult to deal with – but told him he wasn't dead. If he felt pain, he was alive, and he could do something about it.

Or so he told himself.

He sat up, rubbing his forehead.

He looked around.

He was back again. Back in the room with no end. Without any objects. He wasn't even sure if it was a floor he was sitting on. It was just absence – bright, shining absence. There were no walls, no end, no ceiling, no floor, just bright shining nothing.

And it made him want to lurch.

He stood. Looked around himself.

Right.

Come on.

There has to be an exit. *If there is a way in, there has to be a way out.*

He ran. In no particular direction, but in one straight line.

He ran, picked up the pace, sprinted, surged forward – and he just ended up nowhere.

April.

O'Neil was going after April.

It wasn't O'Neil.

How could he be so stupid?

How could he not see it?

Stupid. So stupid. Ridiculous. Pathetic.

A journey around the world and he'd learnt nothing.

You trust no one. Ever.

April.

He went to fall to his knees and chose not to. He wasn't going to collapse in despair, he was going to remain upright and fight. He was going to battle until the end. Be Heaven's warrior. Do everything he could to ensure that no harm came to April – or Julian.

He ran again.

Fast. Faster. Sprinting. Aiming forward, keep going forward, surely there must be an end, must be.

He had a stitch.

Doesn't matter.

A stitch is temporary. It hurts, but it's unneeded. A stitch wasn't going to impede him.

So he kept running.

Aiming at nothing in particular, but only because there was nothing to aim at.

His legs tired.

Just got to keep going.

There'll be an exit soon.

There had to be.

There must be.

But it proved pointless.

He brought himself to a stop and looked around. His surroundings were no different than before.

His burst of adrenaline had done nothing.

He screamed. Bent over and bellowed in frustration.

The scream rebounded back against him, echoing off nothing, as if the echo was created manually, intently, as if to taunt him, to worry him, to make him suffer.

He was going to die here.

He knew it.

There was nowhere to go. Nowhere to turn. No way to escape.

This was his death.

The end.

The final curtain closes and the audience applauds.

The final full stop is completed and the writer finishes his work.

The race ends, and the athlete finds that they have lost, and it was not worth it, not any of it, because it's done, and so are they.

Oscar fell to his knees.

No.

Got to stop this.

Got to get up. Got to keep trying. Got to find a way, do something.

But do what?

There was nothing he could keep trying to do. There was no option he could try. If he at least had a task he knew could work, he'd keep trying until it did. But he didn't even have that. He didn't have any option, no task he could undertake. No idea what he could actually do.

Just emptiness.

Running hadn't worked.

What else could he try?

He was hopeless. Completely, utterly hopeless.

As was April. Even Julian.

The two people who remained on Earth, stood between

Hell and the billions of souls that lived their life completely unaware.

April would suffer.

Oscar knew that O'Neil would see to it.

He shook his head.

Closed his eyes.

He was past denial now. Was this bargaining? Acceptance? Was he finally coming to terms with him completely messing everything up and–

Footsteps.

Oscar could hear footsteps.

He lifted his head.

He couldn't believe it.

Salvation.

A man appeared before him, stood still, unperturbed, unaffected.

"Hello, Oscar," said Derek.

33

THE SUNNY SKY BROKE AND GREY CLOUDS CONSUMED IT, disguising the brightness of the day. People who had left their houses in their summer shorts and summer dresses, pleased for the opportunity to enjoy the sunshine, now dispersed with more rapidity than they left with in the morning.

April thought nothing of it.

This was normal for a British day. Besides, she'd seen the weather forecast, she knew it was coming – so she had dressed appropriately. She merely slid her hoodie out of her bag and put it on. As soon as the drips of rain began to land atop her head, she lifted her head up and continued eating her sandwich on the park bench.

She hadn't fed the ducks since she was a child. It seemed strange to be doing it as a woman in her mid-twenties. It was something you'd often see a child doing, or an old lady doing – but rarely someone her age.

Maybe that's why she felt compelled to do it.

To access that innocent thinking. Go back to a time when these worries didn't plague her. Didn't worry her.

Because she felt it.

Oscar.

It was something in her stomach, a distant sickness, a need to gag that came from an inexplicable source.

Could a Sensitive sense another Sensitive in trouble?

It seemed farfetched, even considering what they could already do. They weren't superheroes, they just channelled powers that were already there that they had greater access to.

But it was something she felt. Something she *knew*.

Did she know it?

She was fairly certain.

She took another few slices of her loaf of bread and broke it into bits. She scattered it around her feet, watching the ducks barge each other out the way for their own slice of dinner.

As April watched one particular duck barge three others out of the way and steal their food, she considered how even animals had their jerks.

The thought made her laugh.

But the laugh quickly faded as reality intruded on her peace.

Was Oscar ever coming back?

Was Oscar even still alive?

Something told her he was alive, and that he would come back – but something else told her that it wasn't that simple. That his path had taken him to difficulty, and that he needed her help.

How, though?

How can you help a man who doesn't want to be helped, or even found?

She broke the last of her bread and scattered it away from the jerk-duck, allowing some of the smaller ducks to have a piece. They all deserved to eat, rather than be bullied out of their food. Most of them managed to get a piece before the nasty duck reappeared over their shoulder.

The rain grew heavier. The dampness of her hoodie made it

cling to her arms. It was time to go home.

Oh, how she didn't want to go home.

It was empty. Not just of a companion, but of affection. All those things that had made her want to rush home were now gone. No matter how much she increased the heating, the house would still be cold. Her nights where she'd wake up sweaty with Oscar's arm wrapped around her, she'd now wake up and pull the duvet around her to further contain the warmth.

She stood.

Early evening hung on the air with the smell of fine rain.

A rustle. From over her shoulder.

She turned.

Nothing.

Just the thudding of gentle rain against the path and the river.

She walked on.

Another rustle.

She looked back over her shoulder.

There was something there.

She turned back around and picked up the pace, walking faster, listening intently so she could hear footsteps.

She heard none, but she could feel it.

Like warm breath on the back of her neck, even though her neck was covered with a hood.

She looked over her shoulder once more.

Not every assailant has a face and feet to follow her with.

She put her hand beneath her hoodie and held onto the cross attached to her necklace.

She looked around the park.

There were no pedestrians on the path. No faces in the distance. Even the ducks had gone.

She was all alone.

And she could feel it getting closer.

34

THAT SELFISH BOY.

And Julian was careful to use the word *boy*, not *man* – as a man faced up to his actions. A man confronted the situation and did what he could to rectify, change, or help those involved.

They didn't run away, convincing themselves they were going on some pathetic spiritual journey, convincing themselves they were doing something for the greater good, when what they were really doing was being a coward – a stone-faced, childish, feeble little coward.

To Hell with him.

Julian's loyalty to Oscar had grown in recent years, following Oscar coming through for Julian multiple times – but his deepest allegiance always went to April. And he hated to see what this was doing to her.

Another phone call saw Julian receive the same answer.

"Yes, Oscar was here," they told him.

"And where did he go?"

"We are not permitted to tell you that."

Julian almost launched the phone across the room.

At some point, Oscar had been to the Vatican. He had spoken to those in charge of the Church, those who dictated so much about their lives. Any major incident, the Church would be there to cover it up, ensuring the delicate public wouldn't have their feeble lives affected by reality. No, this way they could just go on living their lives without any knowledge of what lurked around them – in fact, they lived it with more than lack of knowledge, they lived it with ignorance. So many frauds had produced so many sceptics that had produced so many debunkers that even if the authorities of the Church did come clean, there would only be a horde of angry citizens ready to dispel such preposterous claims.

He'd seen psychics masquerading cold reading as the real thing. Claiming they had some way to contact the other side. "Oh, I have a G, it's a G, I think it's for Grandad, has anyone lost a grandad here?" Then a hundred gobsmacked suckers turn to each other in disbelief that this charlatan has managed to figure out that one of the gullible masses in the audience would attribute the death to their own grandfather – a very common occurrence – to the stupidity of the statement made by the so-called psychic.

No, even if the truth was proven, the world would not be ready for it. The false deities had already created too much ambiguous falsehood for that.

"Are you kidding me? Do you know who I am?"

"Yes."

"I am a Sensitive, just like Oscar. We are the same – except I'm vastly more experienced and about ten years older – meaning I am the one who watches over Oscar, brought him into the battle, so you need to tell me where he is, and tell me right now!"

An audible sigh cleared the other end of the line.

"For the last time, Mr Barth, we have told you all we can tell you."

"Yeah. Yeah, you have. Thanks for that. Thanks a bunch."

Julian sent the phone across the room, screaming *"Arse-holes!"* as he did, knowing he hadn't hung up – but also knowing that the mobile phone breaking into multiple parts would have likely ended the call for him.

He kicked a chair.

Punched the wall.

Tore the framed pictures from the shelves.

Why was he so angry about this?

Why had it pushed him so far?

April. That's why.

April was the most important thing in this life besides his calling. The calling that he took very seriously. There had been no namby-pamby – no, "Oh we're going to have a baby because we're trying to be like regular people, oh look at us, we're so in love, mwah, so lovely, so in love, look at us oh look at us oh look at us we're bloody idiots."

He had denied a relationship, denied such frivolities that normal people doused themselves in.

Why?

Because there was more at stake. More than love, more than precious family life, more than all this nonsense Oscar had created with April.

Neither of them seemed to get that.

Their lives came second. This came first.

Oscar's attempt to kill April under duress was unfortunate – exceedingly unfortunate. But it's what happens when you put your life, and your mental health, on the line in every job you take. This world was not created for the weak, or the everyday folk. This was the life of a Sensitive.

The life lived for others, not for oneself.

And he may have claimed he left to discover more about being a Sensitive, and what it meant – but he'd have learnt that just by prioritising his calling over his own selfish existence.

He'd have learnt that by staying, and realising what happened with April was a fleeting part of being what he is, of doing what he was born to do.

Julian leant against a chair, willing his heavily beating heart to subside, urging himself to cool it.

He wondered if Oscar was ever coming back.

He wondered where Oscar was now.

And if Oscar even realised the mess that had been left as a result of his recklessness, whilst he was living it up on his meaningless quest.

He wondered if Oscar even cared.

35

"OSCAR, GET UP," DEREK COMMANDED – THOUGH THERE WAS NO impatience to his command, only a wise authority that compelled Oscar to obey.

"Derek?" Oscar said, not sure if this was real. "Is this really you?"

"This time, it is."

"What do you mean this time?"

"I saw you briefly before. I tried to warn you, but I couldn't. I wasn't allowed. Now I am, and I'm here, but not for long, so we need to work together and do it quickly."

"Do what quickly?"

"Get you out of here."

"But, Derek, I don't understand, what is going on?"

Derek sighed.

"You're under attack. By the fear demon Agramon who has taken O'Neil's body. O'Neil is gone, there is no way to stop him other than kill him."

"I can't kill a man…"

"He isn't a man."

Derek placed a firm hand on Oscar's shoulder. "Everything you have been told is a lie. All of it."

"How could it be? Eddie told me himself, he told me I could have been conceived by Hell, that I could have been–"

"That was not Edward King."

In a sudden thump, Oscar felt immensely stupid.

Of course it wasn't Edward King.

Why would Edward King tell him those kinds of things?

"Who was it then?" Oscar asked.

"Something conjured up to play on your fears. That's what this demon does, Oscar. He finds what you're scared of and he drives you to insanity with it."

"But what about Eddie – or whatever it was – said. About how I could be evil."

"Nonsense. Sensitives have all been conceived by Heaven, that's what makes you a Sensitive. If you were conceived by Hell, you'd have been long gone by now."

Oscar dropped his head and closed his eyes. He couldn't even bear to look at Derek. Couldn't bear to acknowledge his own gullible naivety. It was his own insecurities that had brought him here. His own deep-seated fears that had allowed him to be manipulated into a position where April was now in danger.

April had never been in danger because of Oscar.

And now, because of his unshakable belief that she was, she was in more danger than she had ever been.

"You need to listen, Oscar, and you need to listen carefully as I explain," Derek said, speaking fast. "We don't have time for you to feel like an idiot, so you need to get over it quickly. O'Neil engineered everything."

"But, he was in your journal–"

"No, he wasn't. It was lies. Placed in your path so you would find him of your own accord, giving him more credibility."

"That note by the bell, was that–"

"I don't think you understand what it is Agramon plans to do."

"Then tell me."

Derek looked deep into Oscar's eyes, as if he was trying to figure something out, as if there was an equation that would tell Derek whether Oscar was prepared to hear what he was about to hear.

"You understand what amalgamation incarnation is?"

"Yes."

"Do you understand what mass possession is?"

"I – lots of people who are possessed, I guess?"

"Well, imagine the two put together."

"But we'd just exorcise each–"

"What's the most amount of exorcisms you have gotten through in a month?"

"Er, two, I think."

"That means you can cover twenty-four victims in a year, compared to the amount of possession there is, that maybe leaves ten or twenty you are unable to save."

"Okay…"

"It takes a year or so for the demon to amalgamate, sometimes longer, sometimes not. This means it's very rare, as you catch most of them first."

"I guess."

"Imagine, now, Oscar – and I really need you to listen now – that the number of possessions that occur in a year rises."

"What, like, to a hundred?"

Derek shook his head. "No. Think about thousands. Tens, or hundreds of thousands. You would not manage to get anywhere near enough of them before the demons took their place on this Earth. And you understand what demons do to mankind?"

"I–"

"No act of unspeakable evil can be committed without a

push from a demon. Every unspeakable act of evil ever committed by man, every destructive, genocidal action, has been committed with a gentle nudge from Hell, and those nudges all occurred when there was an excess of demonic possession. And by excess, I don't mean there were ten or twenty more possessions than we could deal with – there were thousands."

"So then, if there were thousands..."

"Unspeakable acts of evil unlike the world has ever seen would occur. Think of the world wars, the Crusades, Cambodia, all the horrific events from our history – all occurring simultaneously. The world would tear itself apart, and Hell would just sit back and watch."

Oscar took a few steps and Derek followed, allowing it all to register, to fill his mind with logic.

"I don't get it, Derek," he said. "What has this got to do with anything?"

Derek stopped Oscar and locked eyes. Derek's face turned more serious than Oscar had ever seen it when he was alive.

"The only reason Hell isn't able to do this is because the Sensitives are here to balance the equation. It would require that balance to be disrupted to allow Hell to open the door."

"But how–"

"You are here. That's one down. All Agramon now has to do is remove April and Julian."

"But aren't there other Sensitives in the world?"

"Yes, but none who know about it, none who are accessing their gifts."

"But April and Julian are strong–"

"So are you. You're perhaps even the strongest. And he put you here within two weeks. Imagine what he could do to the others."

Oscar tried to process this. It was too much.

Why did this have to be up to him?

It was always up to him.

Oscar. Who was tricked because he was so terrified of becoming what he dreaded.

And in doing so, he paved the way to Armageddon.

"So O'Neil is trying to bring about mass possession."

"Yes."

"For mass – whatever it is you call it."

"Amalgamation incarnation."

"And then?"

"Then, Oscar? Then unspeakable acts of humans will wipe the entire race out, and demons will inherit this world."

APRIL QUICKENED PACE.

She could hear it breathing.

Somewhere behind her, hidden by the darkness, concealed by the shadows. Erratic, off-beat, as if each intake of oxygen was a struggle, as if each one required a war to take it.

She tried looking over her shoulder again, but just like before, and the time before that, she saw nothing.

The park had emptied.

When had that happened?

The low light of a late summer evening had arrived, a dark which normally prompted people's journey home. The rain had prompted some movement; but for so many people to make a hasty retreat without her noticing was strange, to say the least.

She was sure she'd seen a couple on a bench – in fact, she was certain, as she recalled looking at them with envy – there had also been a mother pushing a pram, a group of old ladies.

Now they were gone. As if someone had come along and ushered them all out but forgot to tell April.

She couldn't see the entrance to the park. She couldn't see

it, but she knew it was there, around the next corner, waiting for her, longing for her arrival.

The trees seemed to be growing by the second. Although April knew this was all in the anxiety of her mind, it still seemed as if their branches were growing and entwining and encasing the rest of her path in shadow.

Now she could hear a gentle patter of feet. Like wet feet splashing on the floor, disrupting the raindrops, faint but close.

She couldn't run.

If she ran, then maybe they would strike. Maybe that's when they would pounce, and she would be attacked by whatever it was.

No, if she was going to survive whatever was chasing her, she needed to keep walking. Not running. Just walking, as quickly as she could.

A grunt.

She looked over her shoulder.

She saw its shadow. Low and hunched. Behind her. Close enough to reach out and–

Now, she ran.

Ran until she could see the entrance of the park. It was still another half a minute at least, but she could see it.

Her arm reached out for it.

There were people outside it. Walking. Going about their everyday business.

She tried screaming. No one responded.

Its shadow encompassed hers.

Its deep fingernails dug into her back and took her to the ground. The harsh bumps of the wet cement dug into her chest, her face slammed into its rough surface and her knee scraped.

Something was on top of her.

She turned over.

It was as un-humanlike as a human could get. Rat-like

features, crazy eyes, squirming face. It lifted its hands, it nails long and brown, ready to swipe.

Instinctively, she covered her face.

Its nails took apart the fabric of her sleeves, ripping them, decorating her arms in bloody marks.

"Help me!" she screamed.

What was this thing?

Why was it attacking her?

She took her arms away.

Its hand was around her throat.

It was squeezing.

She couldn't breathe.

She punched its arm. Punched and punched. Chopped the elbow. Did all she could. But it just kept babbling nonsensically, drooling over her, adamant about her imminent death.

"Please!" she tried, but her voice only came out in a croak.

Just as she felt her consciousness poise, the creature was swiped away. Kicked onto its back by some cloaked figure.

The figure withdrew a knife and plunged it into the creature's gut, then slid it out and stuck it into the feral monster's throat.

It fell on the floor and suffocated.

April didn't move. Her body was motionlessly tense.

The figure turned and revealed its face. It was a man. From the collar, April could tell he was a priest. Grey hair, roughly spiked, old enough that he should be weary from such excitement.

"Please, don't be afraid," he said, his voice thick with Irish accent.

"Who– who–" April stuttered.

"His name was Ardal. He used to be a man, but he's beyond that term now."

April looked to the corpse, to the man, grateful for him saving her, terrified that he killed it.

"We need to get out of the park before anything else tries to get you. Is there somewhere we can go?"

"Who are you?" April asked.

"Oh, I am sorry, where are my manners?" The man reached out a hand, took April's, and helped her up. "My name is Father Connor O'Neil, and Oscar sent me to help you."

"So you see," said Derek, "This is far bigger than you or me."

"I don't care," Oscar confidently replied. "Don't get me wrong, I'll get to saving the world, I'll do what I can – but first, April."

Derek bowed his head.

"What?" Oscar asked.

Derek kept his head bowed. Oscar could tell he was hiding something. Something about April.

"What is it?" Oscar demanded.

Derek raised an arm in a prompt for Oscar to wait.

"Is she okay?"

Derek lifted his head.

"No," he answered.

"No? What do you mean no?"

"He's just made contact. Agramon is with her now. It's just a matter of time."

"I've got to get out! I've got to leave and get to her, I have to save her, I can't let him hurt her!"

Derek looked to his right, to his left, and back at Oscar, as if indicating the surroundings.

"Okay," Derek said. "Go on then. Go to her."

Oscar frowned, flinging his arms to the side, his frustration spilling over into hysteria.

"How?"

"I don't know that."

"But I thought you came here to help me!"

"I came here to warn you, to tell you the truth. You got yourself into this predicament. Don't expect me to release you from it."

"But, Derek–"

"I don't have much longer. It took a lot for me to be granted permission to come here, and if I don't return soon, the door will close, and I too will be stuck here forever."

"That's fine, I know what I need to know about what's happening, fine, I just – I need to know how to get out."

Derek shrugged.

"Stop shrugging! Don't you even have an idea? A clue? Anything?"

Derek didn't answer. He just smiled. Keeping his frustrating air of calmness, exuding nothing but control – as he did in life, and now in death.

"Please, Derek. You've got to help me."

Derek placed a hand on Oscar's shoulder.

"What makes you think you need my help?" Derek asked.

"Are you kidding? There's hardly a door marked exit, is there? I could do with some directions."

Derek chuckled.

"Stop it!"

"Stop what, Oscar?"

"Being so – so frigging calm. It's annoying me."

"Maybe if you were a little calmer, the path would present itself a little clearer."

"Great, more cryptic messages, just what I need."

"Oscar–"

"Derek, please, tell me."

Derek looked Oscar dead in the eyes and grinned. "Like I said, Oscar. What makes you think you need my help?"

"Because I have no idea how to get out of here."

"Sure you do. You're a Sensitive."

With that, Derek took his arm away from Oscar, stepped backwards, and grew fainter.

"Oh, please don't go now, Derek."

"You know everything you need to know," Derek said, his parting words growing quieter. "Now use it."

"Derek, please."

Derek's body faded until it was just an outline, then fell to the ground like a pile of sand.

"Derek…"

Oscar was left gaping at the space where Derek had stood.

The sight of him had given Oscar so much reassurance; now what? He'd been told what the stakes are, and he was still stuck there – he was practically in a worse position than he was before.

Oscar looked around himself.

The same endless enclosure remained.

You know everything you need to know. Now use it.

What the hell did that mean?

Why couldn't anyone just tell things to him straight?

If he'd wanted a bunch of unhelpful answers, he would have just stayed at home and asked Julian.

He huffed. Closed his eyes.

Focus.

What else had Derek said?

What makes you think you need my help?

Another useless rhetorical question.

You're a Sensitive.

A Sensitive.

He was a Sensitive.

What did that mean?

Oscar opened his eyes.

You're a Sensitive.

Derek's most vital words. The most obvious, yet the most unthought of.

The whole question he'd been asking, the answers he'd been seeking, laying before him, just out of reach.

You're a Sensitive.

Did that mean he could exert some power here?

Was that the answer to escaping?

THE MAN WHO CALLED HIMSELF FATHER CONNOR O'NEIL SAT coolly at the table that April had sat at so many times with Oscar, either sharing late-morning breakfast or dinner, or just an in-depth conversation.

She tried to distract herself from such memories by focussing on making the drinks. It was only when she went to pour the kettle into the final mug that she realised she'd taken Oscar's favourite mug out too. It had a picture of a Mr Men on it, *Mr Silly* – a big orange top hat out over a yellow cartoon character with excessively large feet. She put it back in the cupboard, behind all the other mugs.

She placed a weak coffee down for herself, a strong coffee for Julian, and a tea with four sugars for O'Neil.

"Thank you," O'Neil said. "You're too kind."

He sipped on it straight away, which was strange, as the water had only just come out the kettle, and April couldn't imagine being able to sip something so hot so soon.

"Father, you said you had news on Oscar," Julian said, always about business, always direct to the point. Sometimes it was a huge annoyance – but, right then, it was hugely helpful, as April was eager to find out where her estranged boyfriend had been.

"Ah, yes. You are definitely Julian. He told me about you."

"He did?"

"Yes, he did. Always curt and straight to the point. Never misses a trick, never dances around a subject, always hits the nail on the head – no, more than hits it, batters it. Bashes it into the wall until the nail is firmly in."

April and Julian forced an appreciative, if impatient, smile.

"That's me," Julian said, his face stern, doing his best to keep cool. April appreciated his support and, despite his and Oscar's rocky relationship, appreciated how much he wanted to track Oscar down too.

"You, April, you're a little different. He told me many a thing about you. Some of it wonderful. Some of it not."

"Oh?"

"He said you were beautiful, eyes that could turn a man to stone – and I see that, oh, I do. He told me you are his strength, the reason he searches for his answers, and the reason he goes on."

"He did?" April said, overjoyed and relieved to hear Oscar still spoke of her in such a way.

"Yes, but he also said there were downsides to your character. As I guess there are in all of us."

"Oh?" April replied, her mood depleted, fighting a tinge of dismay.

"He said you were weak. That you let a baby into you, and let it put you in a hospital bed. He said better women would not have let such things happen."

April didn't know what to say.

She couldn't imagine Oscar ever saying such things about her.

Then again, she couldn't imagine Oscar ever leaving her for

months without any affirmative contact or update on where he was or what he was doing.

Was that really what he thought of her?

After all this time, he thought of her as a pathetic, weak little girl, who struggled so much with life?

"You said you had seen him," Julian said, bringing the conversation directly back to the information they wished to know. "That you could tell us where he was."

"Yes. Last I heard, he was in the Vatican."

April shared a surprised glance with Julian.

"In Rome?" Julian said. He already knew this.

"Yes, in Rome. Though he left shortly after. He went there to ask some questions and – well, I'm not sure he liked the answers."

"Did he," April tried, then rethought her words. "I mean, at any point, did he say anything about when he might be coming home?"

"Home?" O'Neil said, looking confused.

"Yes, home. Back here."

O'Neil smiled patronisingly, as if April was an inept dog unable to fetch a ball back for the owner.

"Oh, my dear, I don't think you understand."

"Understand what?" she said blankly.

"Oscar is home."

Uncomfortable silence settled over the table. April knew Julian was looking at her, but she couldn't return the stare, couldn't share the look. Couldn't acknowledge that Oscar would have left permanently, because it wasn't possible to be thought of – Oscar was coming back. He'd said it. Well, not said it, but implied it – he was going to get answers, then when he had them, he was coming back home, to her.

"In Rome?" Julian asked.

"Sorry?"

"You said last you heard of him he was in Rome, implying

that he wasn't anymore. So is it Rome he considered to be home?"

O'Neil momentarily looked to be caught off guard, but he quickly regathered himself.

"When I spoke to him, yes. But you have to understand, this was a good few weeks ago."

"So for all you know, he might not even be in Rome now?"

"Oscar spoke to me at great length. It seemed he thought I could give him some of the answers he did seek; I gave it a good craic, of course. I did best I could. But in conversation, he asked if I would return to you to relay a message. To give you something."

"What?" April hastily prompted. "What did he give you?"

"Ah, I wrote it down somewhere," O'Neil answered, searching himself. He looked in his trouser pockets, his coat pockets, but it wasn't until his hand found his way to his inside pocket that he found it.

"This," O'Neil said, placing a folded piece of paper on the table. "He had me write this, then pass it on to you."

O'Neil finished his tea and stood.

"I wish you all the best, and I'm sorry I couldn't be of more help."

April went to stand.

"Oh, please don't bother yourself seeing an old man out. I've walked through many doorways, I'm sure I'll manage."

They both stared at the folded note, half-listening to O'Neil's steps through the hallway and opening and closing of the door.

April went to take the note, but Julian abruptly held her wrist.

"Are we sure about this?" he said.

"What?"

"We've been fooled before. We all have."

"Now's not the time, Julian."

"You're vulnerable. To them, this is the perfect time."

"Julian, if this is from Oscar, I need to see it. And O'Neil is a priest." Her eyes made Julian weak. They pleaded with him longingly, months of pain presented through her hardened exterior, the exterior Julian could always see through so well.

"Fine," Julian said, taking his hand away.

April opened the folded note.

Gazed at it.

Looked to Julian.

"Have you got your car?" she asked.

"Yes, why?"

April presented the folded note, and the few lines written upon it.

"It's an address. Let's go."

I'm a Sensitive.

I'm a Sensitive.

I'm a Sensitive.

But what did that even mean?

Oscar screamed into the eternal barrenness. The everlasting desolation.

If he knew what that meant, he would never have had to start this stupid voyage. He'd never have abandoned April, he'd never have ended up in this position, and he'd never have allowed himself to be fooled so damn easily.

He sat down, covering his face with his hands, and let his energy give out as he collapsed onto his back. He remained laying there, floating on the blank space, staring up at…

What?

What was he looking at?

There was nothing even there.

I'm a Sensitive

I'm a Sensitive.

I'm a Sensitive.

But so what?

The vacancy before him was untouched. Unblemished.

A blank canvas.

In his mind, he painted that canvas. Covered it in pictures of what could be. What should be. The ideal version of events, if things had happened the way they should have.

Pregnancy.

April and Oscar's happiness progressing through nine months without worry. Without having to torment themselves with paranormal births or supernatural entities plaguing her body.

The birth.

To an actual human baby child.

April would not be comatose and debilitated following the birth. She'd be tired, yes, of course – but she'd be happy. The doctor would hand the baby to Oscar and he'd hold back tears of joy. They'd both gaze upon the face of this gift – not a gift in the way that him being a Sensitive is a gift – but a gift in the sense of something that has graced their life with positivity, something that has eternally changed them for the better.

She'd grow to a toddler age, and maybe they'd think about getting married.

Their daughter would be a bridesmaid – young, but suitably perfect for the role. Julian would be his reluctant best man. Or hell, maybe Julian would give April away.

Then you'd be pronounced man and wife.

Then you'd kiss.

And then you'd be happy.

Not in a happy-ever-after kind of way – Oscar had always been sceptical about those kinds of endings. He always thought – what happens after the happy ending?

But for them, the happy ending would just be the start of their story.

Then you'd have another child. Maybe even twins.

Then you'd find others who are dormant Sensitives. Teach

them to harness their powers. Maybe have a school or a department in a university, train the next generation, until there are enough that no one need put themselves at the kind of risk the three of them had in the past few years.

There would be no mass possession.

The quantity of Sensitives would be such that amalgamation incarnation would be something taught in a history lesson.

And April and Oscar would grow old.

They would grow old and die happy, reflecting on a full life lived.

He wiped the canvas away.

It wasn't going to happen. It was never going to happen.

But they could still paint this canvas. Just with something else.

April and Oscar could still grow old together, but the happiness could be from avoidance of insanity. Of facing what they face and still being in love.

Being strong together.

Because maybe that's what being a Sensitive is.

It's about sacrificing the ideals. About stripping away the decorations of life that you don't need and doing what is important.

Oscar can still have April, and April can still have Oscar.

But the world would need them to fight.

And in that sense, they would have to be selfless.

Maybe that was the answer.

That selfish thoughts were burdens. Happiness was earnt through hard work, not a given right.

Their love would survive in the knowledge that they had been put on this Earth for something more than the average person.

They had been put on the Earth to prevent what O'Neil was bringing about.

I am a Sensitive.

I am a Sensitive.

I. Am. A. Sensitive.

I am meant for something more.

My actions have been selfish.

In a wave of clear thought, he closed his eyes, and realised his own failings.

I am a Sensitive. I am a soldier. And my life is meant for this.

His life was meant for this.

Suddenly, he wasn't scared anymore.

That fear that he would hurt April – it was unfounded. Illogical.

They would get hurt.

But their strength would be what protected them. Their love for each other would ensure that they fought by each other's side without ever surrendering for one another.

He wasn't going to hurt her.

She wouldn't let him.

But even if he did hurt her, or she hurt him – they would always be there to stop the other.

And in one illuminating, mind-blowing epiphany, he realised:

I am a Sensitive. And I'm not scared any more.

He opened his eyes.

He lay on a stone floor. Pitch-black. Cold moisture hung in the air.

The eternal nothing was gone. The room at the end of the tunnel beneath the church was back.

I did it.

He leapt to his feet.

He hadn't a moment to waste.

But he wasn't alone

Something was there in the darkness, heavy breathing,

growling, something that was only just noticing Oscar's newfound presence.

Beside his feet he felt something solid. Something robust.

He lifted it up.

It was O'Neil's flashlight.

He switched it on.

Three familiar figures blocked his way. Three figures hunched over, drooling, spitting, snapping, rambling, freed from restraints and ready for the kill.

Of course, he wouldn't be allowed to leave so easily. There would be a backup. An assurance that Oscar couldn't escape.

And that assurance was left in the bodies of three former exorcists, three former sufferers from demonic possession, three people Oscar had seen in the institution.

Except, they weren't people anymore, were they?

The people who were born into those bodies were long gone. What Oscar was facing was three demons in their prisoners' skin.

40

HE WATCHED AS THOSE PATHETIC LITTLE BEETLES SCUTTLED INTO the imminent death with the gullibility of a three-year-old child.

Honestly, an eternity of watching these pathetic morsels – *people* – going about their little lives like they think there is something grander had made him bored of the species; yet, at the same time, their stupidity never ceased to amaze him.

The address was perfect.

It was just a house.

To them, anyway.

To him, it was a hive of evil. It was a place he'd spent time bewitching, cursing, infiltrating with every evil incantation and every sickening presence and every spiteful spirit he could until it was full – full to the brim and bursting – with enough to entrap them and keep them in there until they burst with terror.

Hell saw a fear demon as the easiest of demons – the route was so easy. Hell approached the succubae and demons of illness with far more respect; those were things that took work, so they said, things that took multiple enchantments and the right victim. Preying on a human's fear was like preying on the sea to have waves in a storm. It hardly even took a nudge.

He had proven otherwise.

Yes, it was simple enough to play on someone's fears and watch them suffer. To possess someone and remain unnoticed as they pushed each fear to the forefront of their mind until you picked the right moment and snatched their body, snatched it away from them, with the work done before the demon even reveals itself.

To take the three Sensitives – the three who guarded the world from Hell, though they didn't seem to realise it – and to force them into insanity through tricks of the mind was not easy.

In fact, this had been the biggest challenge he'd faced in his thousands of years corrupting the earth's mongrels. But, with the satisfaction it gave him, it had turned into the easiest.

They don't even know, do they?

That this Earth did not belong to them.

Once, Hell was left free to roam the Earth. Hell wasn't needed – demons took their place before any conscious mind did. Humans go about their lives thinking dinosaurs are the only thing that predates them.

There is evil that exists that predates even life itself.

But the evidence isn't as forthcoming as bones in the ground. It's left in the remnants of destruction.

And soon Lucifer will hail this fear demon as the one deserving of a title as prince of Hell – no, *prince of Earth* – because they will need Hell no more.

The woman and the man pulled up outside the house.

They got out, walked up to it, like they would any resi-dence; even with everything they've seen, they still approached with the stupidity and naivety and innocence and downright belligerent denial the human race had become accustomed to.

The man looked anxious. He held onto her arm, told her to hang back. He was suspicious.

O'Neil had played his part, but had he tried to play it too well?

Ah well, O'Neil wasn't needed anymore.

People won't be needed as conduits for demons. Demons will rise, and the humans will pray to them – and mercy will not be forthcoming.

Still they entered, this man and woman, these two Sensitives; personifying the mortal foolishness they represent.

They entered through the same door, but little did they know, they'll be in a separate house.

The same, physically, yes.

But the charms would work. They have been years in the making. He'd planned for this moment; he'd planned for the Sensitive's frivolousness. He expected it.

No one else did.

But he had.

And now it came to fruition.

They entered through the same door.

And it has begun.

All he needed to do now was wait.

In just hours, the brick wall between Hell and Earth would falter.

The possession would increase.

The amount of souls that were banished out of their body whilst the demons amalgamated would grow.

The human atrocities would surge.

And then the demons would rise, like they did when the Antichrist gave them entry.

They will wipe them out with the swipe of their hand.

It will be like picking heads off flowers.

Watching the petals fall off, knowing that it was helpless.

They would be the ant beneath the magnifying glass. Burning them with the flames of Hell.

A flick of the grin, and an imminent shedding of the skin.

He could feel it.

The future.

Soon that future was going to become *now*.

THE HOUSE HAD BROWN BRICK, A PERFECTLY TRIMMED GARDEN with flourishing flowers, and a painted door displaying a house number left wide open. A people carrier was on the drive, a basketball net above the garage, and children's toys scattered across the lawn, as if they were used so much there was no need to put them away. The smell of a roast dinner greeted them, along with the sound of a child's television show being played too loud from the living room.

This was the kind of house April could have shared with Oscar. She didn't voice this to Julian, but he knew what she'd be thinking.

They entered without reservation.

"Hello?" April offered.

As soon as their feet were placed on the carpet, the door slammed shut. The light dimmed. All noises ceased. The roast dinner no longer wafted its welcoming odour, replaced instead by the smell of damp and rotting food. The house's temperature plummeted, prickling her arms, forcing her breath to form in clouds.

She turned to Julian beside her.

But there was no one beside her.

She turned to leave – but there was no door handle. She pushed it, tried to pull its hinges, but it didn't falter, as solid as the wall that surrounded it.

She pressed herself up against this functionless door as she turned and surveyed the room she was in. The corridor had narrowed and extended, the walls so close she would be unable to hold her arms out wide. The plaster was full of cracks, the floor lined with dust, all light escaped.

Except for the light at the end of the corridor.

A distant room.

She turned back to the door. Tried it again.

She hit it. Bashed it. Screamed, hollered, made as much noise as she could, shouted for help, beckoned for Julian.

It was useless.

She stopped and leant her head against the door, buried in her arms, refusing to sob, refusing to cry.

How could she be so foolish?

How could she not–

"April…"

Her melancholy self-deprecating rambles ceased, her mind falling silent.

Something said her name, almost in a singsong, but so quiet it could have been a whisper.

She turned and looked over her shoulder.

The far room. Lit by lamplight. There was movement. Something was there.

"April…"

It came again.

This time the voice was more distinguishable. It had more character – it was a male voice, one that felt familiar, one that belonged to…

"April…"

Oscar.

Was he here?

Or was this her in denial?

Was this just another trap?

But what else was there to do – there was no way out. This was her only option.

But her legs would not move.

She was rendered manically immovable. Unable to act, unable to stop questioning everything. Every move she could make, every action she could take, she second-guessed and ridiculed herself for thinking it in the first place.

"April… Come on…"

"Oscar?" she tried. "Oscar, is that really you?"

No. It can't be.

"Come on, April…"

She took a step forward. Placed her arms on the walls, the rough plaster digging into the tender skin of her palm, her fingers gliding along the jagged edges of its broken points.

She took another step, and another, and another.

Then she stopped.

That was far enough.

"Oscar, can you hear me?"

She waited.

And waited.

Wishing he would reply, and in a way that made sense, that meant she could be sure it was him – which of course, it obviously wasn't – but what if it was?

That burning longing she had buried deep inside her resurfaced, and whether it was Oscar or just something pretending, she still wanted to run toward it just so she could smell his deodorant or feel the thickness of the back of his hair.

But she had to be sensible.

Had to think this through.

"Oscar?"

Another step.

And another.

And another.

"Oscar, is that really you?"

She looked behind her. The door and the room were now of equal distance. She could run back, or she could go forward.

She talked herself into confidence.

She was a Sensitive, for Christ's sake. She'd had evil spirits channel through her multiple times. She'd survived numerous demonic attacks, and she had come out relatively unscathed – physically, anyway.

She could take this.

Whatever it was, she could take this.

"Oscar, I'm coming."

She walked forward, this time with a little more speed, steadying her shaking legs with her arms against the walls.

She reached the doorway and she paused. Nothing but the lamplight before her.

"April, come on."

She couldn't see him.

Why couldn't she see him?

"April, come on, we're just around the corner."

She stepped into the room.

As soon as she did, a huge thud came from behind her.

She turned around. The hallway had gone. Replaced by solid wall.

She was in her living room.

With Oscar.

There he was. Sat on the floor, his back to her.

"Oscar?"

He turned his head to look at her. His face was the same, his arms the same. It was him. Smiling at her like he'd never been away.

She wanted to run up to him and hug him, kiss him, tell him how much she missed him and how much she needed him.

But something stopped her.

He had something on his lap.

Some*one* on his lap.

As he shifted his body, that someone became clear.

She crumbled to her knees. Looking from his face to hers, from reassuring smiles to those same sick, sadistic eyes.

"Hello, Mummy," said Hayley. "Have you come to play?"

42

THREE ON ONE.

Those weren't Oscar's choice of odds.

They all circled around him, dripping bloody saliva, hunch-backed, growling. Each a different demon in a human body, each a different victim that had been beaten, each a person that had failed to be saved.

Oscar had fought the demonic in many ways – but never in an actual, physical fight. He was a skinny, scrawny guy who'd never set foot in a gym. He was hardly someone who could take on three feral creatures ready to rip him apart with their teeth.

So why weren't they attacking?

Why were they waiting?

Oscar, somehow instinctively, reached into his pocket.

His crucifix.

He withdrew it.

But surely – that couldn't be why they weren't attacking?

Any normal demonic possession, yes – but not three severe cases of amalgamation incarnation? Oscar's understanding was that once a demon had taken a human's place on Earth, religious items didn't have the same effect.

He reached the crucifix toward them.

They didn't flinch.

Yet they didn't attack.

"So you got out, then?"

A woman's voice. A figure down the dank, dark corridor, behind the three figures.

Oscar directed the torchlight at the voice.

Another strange occurrence – if he only had one source of light, why weren't those three demons killing it? His crucifix wasn't protecting the light, after all.

Unless they weren't meant to kill him.

Unless they were just meant to keep him there.

"I hope that Eddie at least gave you some answers."

He recognised the voice.

And, as soon as he recognised it, he couldn't believe what a fool he was.

"Hazel."

"I suggest you listen to him."

"What, to Eddie? You mean the fake image of Eddie you somehow conjured up?"

"Who told you it was fake?"

"Someone much wiser."

"Then I would suggest you adjust your perception of what is fake and what isn't. Maybe *he* was the fake one, and what we showed you was the truth."

"Yes, but–"

Whoa.

Stop.

Hang on.

That's it…

But surely not? This couldn't be true…

It seemed so simple. Yet, at the same time, such monumental complexity – how had he managed to produce this?

Agramon. The fear demon.

That's how.

Hazel emerged fully into the light.

"You know, it would be much easier if you took your own life – and we are willing to give you that chance, before I let my three friends here off the leash."

Oscar laughed.

Having realised what he had just realised, such a suggestion seemed ridiculous.

"Oh, are you?"

"You laugh, but I suggest you take this choice."

"And is it in the remit of a demon to grant mercy? I've never witnessed that before."

"I would–"

Oscar threw the crucifix at her.

It went straight through her and clattered off the far wall.

He looked at the three people circling him – the three projections of fear – and rued his own lack of foresight.

"I get it now," Oscar said.

"You do?"

"These three – they were part of my fear. They were meant to be what I'm scared I could become. You – well, you were my fear of the life I could never have with April. I thought it weird that you would invite some random guy on a park bench to go have dinner with your family."

"I–"

"You wanted to show me what I thought I could never have with April." He took another step toward her. "You wanted that fear to grow. That I would fall victim to demonic possession through my own vulnerability as a Sensitive, that I would destroy that family – so clever. So simple."

"You will not leave this room."

"Yeah, I think I will."

Oscar directed the flashlight toward his exit and walked straight through her, and straight through one of the three creaturesque figures that seemed so silly and pathetic now.

"You won't win," Hazel claimed.

Oscar collected his crucifix en route to the exit and placed it neatly back in his pocket.

"It's useless," Hazel insisted. "If he doesn't kill April, you probably will."

"No," Oscar said, in his final glance back before he pulled himself out of the pit. "I won't."

43

NOTHING MOVED FAST ENOUGH.

In a city that was always moving, it all suddenly seemed to slow down.

The taxi drivers who normally swung you round corners and bustled to get in front of slower vehicles – where were they? Because the taxi driver that drove Oscar insisted on going slower than most, and it only exacerbated Oscar's temperament even further.

"Can we go a little quicker?" he'd prompted, his leg bouncing, moving from one window to the other, willing the traffic to part.

"Don't worry, you'll make your train."

How the hell would he know? He had no idea when Oscar's train was!

Honestly, neither did Oscar. His instinct had been to get to the station and hope for the best.

Once he arrived, Oscar threw a handful of money to the driver and leapt onto the street. He went down the stairs, not caring about who he barged out the way or how many people swore at him for his haste.

He had to get back. He had to be home. April was in danger. Julian was in danger.

If Derek's knowledge was reliable, then O'Neil had already got to them.

They could already have been trapped in a whirlwind of insanity, driven out of their minds by manipulation of their fears, forced to the very edge of their rationality and made to abandon all reason.

The only real reassurance Oscar had as he sprinted through gaps was that April was strong – which she was. She was incredibly strong. Admirably so. The strongest person Oscar knew, and that was what made him love her so much.

Then that irritating thought buzzed over his reassurance: *it worked on me.*

Not that he was anywhere near as strong as April, but he was a Sensitive, and he knew as much as she did about the world they fought.

A train to Cheltenham, Gloucestershire, was parting in one minute. Platform 8. He could already see the train waiting through the window.

He raced to the stairs, leapt down them three at a time, barged a young couple out of the way, ignoring their retaliation. It didn't matter. Their protests were irrelevant.

If they weren't going to tolerate his barging for April's sake, they would have to put up with it for the fate of the world.

The thought almost slowed him down.

The fate of the world.

The survival of his species.

That was what was resting on this now. Not the soul of a possessed victim, but the souls of every man, woman and child on this Earth.

He made it to the train. He found a seat, fell into it, and closed his eyes, willing himself to calm as much as he could.

His heart. His breathing. His perspiration.

Everything was shooting ahead.

And this train was still static. Why was it so static? It needed to move, hurry, get there as quick as it could.

That's when Oscar realised he had a four-hour train journey ahead of him.

This adrenaline he felt, the desperation, all of it, he was going to have to bury for the proceeding two hundred and forty minutes.

That would be the hardest part.

Having to sit there, unable to do anything, unable to act in any way that would make the journey faster.

He could urge the driver to move – but say what? That Hell was converging with Earth to remove people and replace them as the dominant life on this planet?

Even he thought he sounded ridiculous, and he knew it was the truth.

No, he was going to have to force patience. Even if patience was the last thing he could access at that moment, he was going to have to force it, like a nail through a solid stone wall – he had to hammer that patience into himself.

His breathing was still rushing ahead of his lungs, still lurching through his throat. A hoarse cough spluttered through his mouth and he did all he could to concentrate, to calm himself.

The train began to move, alleviating a small amount of his tension. But he knew this was just the start of his journey – he had a while to wait, to sit and think about what was happening to April whilst he was sat, panicking on a train.

A child was staring at him.

Oscar didn't blame the kid.

His hands were gripping the side of his seat, his entire body tensed, his breathing moving quickly in and out.

He'd probably stare at himself if he could.

Then the child's mother turned him around, offered him

some food, and their father made sure he had everything he needed for the long trip ahead.

The thought struck him with the most clarity it ever had: *that is going to be me and April someday.*

Never before had the thought seemed more possible and impossible at the same time.

44

SOMEONE, SOMEWHERE SCREAMED. APRIL WAS FAIRLY CERTAIN IT was her, though she couldn't be sure. She couldn't be sure of anything.

"Mummy, what's wrong?"

"Stop – stop it…"

"Mummy?"

"Stop calling me Mummy!"

Hayley looked confused. She looked to her father, a face of perplexity warranting an answer.

"I think Mummy is just a little confused right now," Oscar told her.

April backed away, searched for the door, but it had gone, melded into the outline of her living room. Her living room as it was before Oscar left, full of vibrancy and colours, well-kept. Along the floor, scattered toys and colouring books – but they had been placed too perfectly. These weren't the discarded playthings of a child, they were the particularly placed ornaments of a scene, a stage decorated.

"It's not you," April said, mostly to herself, in a whisper that was lost in the child's laughter.

"Oh, Mummy, stop it!"

April couldn't bear it. She had to turn away. False or not, whatever this was, it was the very thing that had driven Oscar away from her, the very thing that had been the source of her pain and her condition and had threatened the very life she held.

This thing could not be allowed to survive in any form.

"Mummy," said the voice, closer.

April turned her face to see Hayley tugging on her jeans.

"Mummy, what's the matter?"

"Get off me!" she wailed, and pushed the child away.

"April, what the hell are you doing?" Oscar demanded, leaping to his feet.

April ran over to the kitchen drawer, found a knife, took it, and charged at Hayley. Her eyes full of fire, her voice breaking against the constraints of her scream, she plunged the knife through the air, only to be met by Oscar's strong hand around her wrist.

"You…" he said, squinting evilly into her eyes, staring into her mind with eyes of hate and retaliation.

"Oscar, please…"

She knew it wasn't him.

She was sure of it.

So why did she still keep calling him by his name?

Oscar's hand lifted her wrist, pushing the knife closer to her own throat.

"Oscar, you promised this would never happen again."

"That was before you tried to hurt my child."

She tried to pull away from the knife that slowly meandered toward her, ignored the crumple of Oscar's angry face – and beyond them, at the end of the room, she saw Julian.

"Julian!" she cried.

Julian simply shook his head.

"Julian? Where have you been? Please help me!"

"Why would I save you?"

"What?"

"You were a piece of scum when I picked you off the street, and you stayed like that ever since."

"Julian, please."

The knife edge pressed against her throat.

"No."

Julian turned and left, somehow, despite a solid wall standing in his way, he still evaporated through it.

The knife pierced her skin. She felt herself draw blood.

"Please, Oscar. I love you."

"You love me?" he mocked.

She pushed him off and clambered over the kitchen table, falling to her knees, collapsing on her back, her hand over her neck, covering the faint wound, pressing against the slight bleed, the injury that, should the knife have been pressed further, would have proven fatal.

She closed her eyes.

Wished she wasn't there.

Wished it was just a dream.

Opened them.

She was somewhere else. The kitchen table, the walls, the living room, the dining room, everything had gone. She was sat up on the floor of a house, but she wasn't there. Yet she was.

She understood this sensation. She understood what it was.

Her body was acting as a conduit.

Only, her body was no longer being used. It was being taken over. She would normally still have her fingertips pressed around her flesh – but now, she couldn't feel anything.

She looked down, and there she was.

Her body. Her eyes closed. Someone speaking through her.

This wasn't how it went. This wasn't how it was supposed to go.

Her own eyes opened and looked at her, a maleficent grin from cheek to cheek, the eyes of someone she'd channelled.

"I got your body…" the version of herself sang – as if it was an adult playing I-got-your-nose with a child.

And, no matter how hard she tried, she could not return to that body.

She'd lost it.

Was this Hell?

Julian had never been, but he'd read Derek's journals, and he'd heard stories by those few who had been and returned.

Stories had recounted it as a place of fire, pits of lava spewing over molten rock, sickening laughter of demons you can't see, distant screaming of people hidden away.

And this was where he was.

Laying on the rocky surface of a giant lump of stone, remaining in the centre to avoid the lashes of lava from grabbing him.

He sat up, rubbed his head.

He'd been fighting for what felt like hours, but he'd lost, and this was where he ended up. Whatever demon he'd fought had been too strong and they had condemned him to an eternity of servitude.

There was someone else.

He stood.

On a large piece of rock, maybe a few yards away across the lava, a figure, a woman, laying on her back, her feet toward him. Her face was on the slope of the far end, he couldn't see it perfectly.

He didn't want to see it perfectly.

He saw the spreading of purple hair down the woman's shoulders.

But he had to see.

He had to know.

"April?" he shouted.

She didn't move. Didn't falter. Didn't flinch.

That's when he noticed – she didn't breathe.

He took a few paces back, readied himself for a run up, took a few strides and – stopped himself. It was too far. Just too far.

No, it wasn't too far.

He tried again, going back, stretching, galloping the few paces he had and leaping across to the other rock, landing on his knees, cutting them but not caring.

It was her.

The lava melted away, the fire pushed into clumps of ash and separated into a field, a grave on a mound, where Julian knelt, her still in his arms.

Before him, the tombstone.

He didn't need to look at it to know the name.

"Well," said Oscar.

Derek looked up to see Oscar's cocky face and folded arms standing over him.

"What do you want?" Julian grumbled.

"I left her alone with you and you killed her."

"I killed her?"

"Pitiful."

"Where the hell have you been?"

Oscar chuckled. A cocky chuckle that only incensed Julian further.

He let April go and sprang to his feet, his fist raised to

Oscar, and he fell to nothing. He looked up and Derek's study surrounded him.

"You dare show your face here again?" said Derek.

"You're not him," Julian refuted.

"Oh, denial. Your favourite pastime. I knew you were never going to be good enough to do this."

"Shut up."

"Edward King was a better man than you. Martin was a better man than you. *Oscar* is a better man than you."

"I know you're not real."

Derek shook his head.

"There you go again, same old–"

"You don't fool me. I will get out of here. I will beat this. I will win. I always win."

Derek took a step toward Julian, his smile widening further.

"You don't realise," he said. "You've already lost."

4 6

HE STOOD ON THE EDGE OF THE WORLD JUST WAITING TO SEE IT burn. Hot anticipation tingling his weak skin.

They were gone. All three of them, the Sensitives, the guardians. The ones that bring the balance that denies the assault from Hell. Heaven's security against a legion of demons.

Each of them incapacitated. Busy fighting their own fears, falling deeper into insanity.

How easy it had been.

How simple.

So simple it seemed bizarre it had never been attempted before. There had always been attempts, he knew that. The world had never been safe – but a fear demon, the vagabond of the underworld, was now bringing about the end.

Atop the hill edge, he knelt to one knee, bowed his head to the full moon, and prayed to be accompanied.

"Hail, fair god, hail," he said, obedient and sure. "You are alive, hear my call, heed my request."

The devil was always listening.

But he rarely answered.

Only if you showed good cause, good reason, if you demanded his faith, would he show.

Agramon just had to prove it.

"Lucifer, righteous fallen angel, come forth to me and hear my prayer."

A rumble of distant thunder that could be him or could be anything – no concrete response.

Had he not proven himself worthy?

Had he not proven himself able to bring forth what the devil had always wanted?

"Faithful king, please heed my beckon, your path is–"

A gust of wind drew itself along the coast and knocked him off his knee. He gathered himself quickly, standing and brushing dirt off his mortal prison.

What he'd give to be rid of it now. He'd fought for it, but he wanted his opportunity to be on this Earth in his true form. Not encased in someone's leftovers.

So why had he been brushed off his feet? There was no wind around – was this his message?

How could his response be so?

He bowed his head. Closed his eyes.

Yet he could feel it. His work was not done. The balance was still not tilted in their favour.

But how?

The two Sensitives were in the house, they were–

Oscar.

He had escaped. He had overcome it.

How?

A mighteous roar sprang along the vocal cords of this weakening body.

Oscar would be travelling to Cheltenham, he was sure of it. Oscar's priority would be to save his friends, looking for a way to get to them before Agramon got to them first.

That was where he would see Oscar off.

Glory was in his grasp. Eternal damnation was in theirs.

What stood in his way?

A child? A thing with thousands of years in their disadvantage compared to him?

This was a temporary glitch, if that.

It would soon be rectified.

OSCAR WAS ALREADY WAITING BY THE DOORS OF THE TRAIN AS IT arrived on Platform 2. He'd been waiting there ever since he began to recognise the fields firing by the window. There were only two platforms at Cheltenham station, one going north and one going south – and Oscar had visited this station enough times to know which side he was going to end up.

What he wasn't expecting was to see O'Neil's smug face amongst the crowd waiting on the platform, standing still as people fled off the train amid rush hour.

At first, Oscar didn't move.

He just stared, watching O'Neil's static grin stare back at him. O'Neil was stood with his feet shoulder-width apart, arms confidently folded – there was an air of arrogance that had previously been disguised as part of O'Neil's character, and Oscar was finally starting to see the real traits of the demon.

And a demon's biggest trait is deception.

He had to make sure not to be fooled.

So what next?

He knew he had to get to April – and Julian. But he also

knew O'Neil wouldn't be stood on the train platform for no reason.

The train emptied. The rush of people left the platform and the train left the station. Besides a handful of commuters sitting on a far bench, they were the only two that remained.

"Oscar!" O'Neil called. "I am not here to hurt you."

Oscar said nothing. Just watched.

"I am here to tell you where April is. If that's what you choose."

It couldn't be that simple.

Oscar wasn't prepared to be fooled again.

"In fact, I'm going to give you a choice. Two, actually. Where one of those is April, and the other will save your world – yet, I already know which one you will choose. That is how confident I am, that I'll give you both choices and let you pick the wrong one."

O'Neil took a step forward.

Oscar's body tensed. His hands balled into fists. He readied himself for a fight.

O'Neil stopped and raised his hands in the air.

"I'm not here to fight. If I was here to fight, we would have fought. I'm here, like I said, to offer you a choice."

"But if you already know which choice I'm going to choose, why would you offer it to me?"

"Because you haven't heard the choice yet. Come."

O'Neil reached Oscar's side and led them up the stairs from the platform. Oscar remained slightly behind O'Neil the whole way, watching every part of his body, particularly the hands, prepared for any movement or attack.

But there was none. The raging demon inside O'Neil's skin appeared surprisingly docile.

Which only made Oscar more on edge.

"I must praise you," O'Neil said. "To begin with, anyway.

Figuring it all out was very wise of you. I didn't give you enough credit."

"Where's April?" Oscar asked as they emerged from the station, crossed the road, and slowly walked down a path beside a moderately busy road and a row of old-fashioned houses. Evenly placed trees decorated their route with beauty, but Oscar did not avert his eyes to admire it. He'd seen those trees plenty of times, he'd lived here his whole life – it was the demon walking beside him he wasn't sure about.

"To figure out, as you must have done, what I managed to conjure up out of your fear and place in your mind – only a true Sensitive could figure such a thing out."

"Where's April?"

"Alas, that does bring us to April – and, unfortunately, I do not think she's figuring it all out with the ease you did."

Oscar stopped, forcing O'Neil to stop, growing angry at the nonchalance of O'Neil's breezy pace and casual attitude.

"Then I'm wasting time, and I need to stop talking to you."

O'Neil withdrew a piece of paper from his pocket.

"On this piece of paper is the address of the house April and Julian are in – though don't expect it to be easy to penetrate. I have spent years putting every hex on it I can, and I–"

Oscar went to snatch the piece of paper, but O'Neil moved it out of reach.

"Ah, ah, ah – you haven't heard the choice yet."

"What choice?"

"And, like I said, the beauty is that I already know which one you will choose – which is why, like a clumsy villain in a bad James Bond story – I always did like those stories – I am going to tell it to you, so I can watch you with smugness as you throw everything away."

"I'm losing patience."

"Okay, okay, Oscar – don't lose it. Your choice is, either you go save April, or you don't."

Oscar raised his arms into the air. "What's the catch?"

"There truly is no fooling you, is there, Oscar?"

Oscar raised his eyebrows expectantly.

"If you go to this address to save April and you enter, then all three Sensitives who keep the balance between Heaven and Hell will be gone – disappeared into the world I have created in this house."

"And?"

"And that is when I will begin unloading from Hell. Without you here, it is our chance, and we *will* take it."

Oscar stared at the piece of paper just out of reach, knowing what he should do, and knowing what he couldn't.

"See, I can already see the decision being made," O'Neil continued.

Oscar wished this was easier.

That he could do what he had to.

But he couldn't.

He just couldn't.

"And there it is," O'Neil – no, *Agramon* – taunted. "You choose her."

"Give me the fucking paper."

O'Neil grinned that same merciless conceited, grin he had when Oscar alighted from the train.

Oscar hated it. Oh, he hated it.

O'Neil held the piece of paper out for him.

"You are truly ready to do this for her?"

Oscar snatched the piece of paper, looked at the address. He knew the street. It was close. He could run.

Without looking back, that's what he did. Run. For his life.

For hers.

Leaving Agramon to begin.

4 8

April was pinned flat against the wall.

Did she do this?

Or was it being done to her?

Where even was she?

She looked down. She was so high up. She couldn't move. Her arms were out like a cross, and every muscle she tried to move fought back against her.

"I'd never love you as much as her," Oscar told her, brushing Hayley's hair.

Hayley's eyes never moved from April's. The whole time they were watching her, locked, staring at her with that smile, that same smile that grin that face those eyes green flickering red flickering red flickering red and why – why – why was this happening?

She thought the girl was dead.

She thought the *demon* was dead.

Oscar said he'd banished it back to Hell. She'd taken Julian to the hospital and he had banished it back to Hell that's what he said that's what he said but *could he be lying?*

April tried to bow her head in shame but even that couldn't move.

"Please…"

"Do you want to do it, Daddy?" Hayley asked, passing him a knife.

"No," Oscar answered, withdrawing his own knife. "We'll do it together."

They hugged, shared their love, shared their embrace and turned and looked at her, both of them peering into her soul into her deep, pitiful soul the man she loved she trusted she hoped would return he returned and now he was going to kill her.

Kill. Her.

"Please…" she begged. Begged, like it mattered, like it did anything, like it ever had – how many times had begging worked? Had a psychopath or sociopath or demon or killer or anyone ever in fact ever turned back on their homicidal intentions for the fact that someone begged?

Hayley and Oscar joined hands.

Walked toward her.

So slowly. As if intentionally. As if the build-up was half the pleasure. As if this walk was cementing the father-daughter bond they felt, off to do something together, they coloured together played toys together now hey, it's time to go kill Mummy, let's kill Mummy – though she wasn't Mummy, she was just a surrogate, a surrogate to a demon who would be killed by her own creation except it wasn't her creation it wasn't even Oscar's it was Hell's and she begged some more.

"Oscar… You love me… Please…"

Who was she trying to convince?

Him?

Herself?

If being a sensitive wasn't enough to stop him, how would love be?

No, he was far too gone this time. He'd fallen down the well and rummaged beneath it, buried himself with the filth that lay beyond the world, beneath the world, in the pits of Hell – that's where this thing had come from, after all.

This thing that wore her face.

But it was wrong. So wrong.

Oscar had resisted killing her before.

But now, as they approached, she was fairly certain she wouldn't get a second chance.

Unlike the second chance she was willing to give to him.

THIS TIME, OSCAR DID USE HIS CRUCIFIX.

It didn't work on those that had already crossed over – there was no protection from Hell for them. But it did work against hexes, enchantments, and spirits. Which, from what he'd already experienced so far, he fully expected this house to be full of.

Strange, it appeared so normal. Child's toys scattered across the garden, budding flowers, a people carrier outside the garage.

It was all lies. All of it.

Oscar may not have known that a week ago, but he damn well knew it now.

Holding his weapon tightly in his hand, the only weapon an exorcist ever truly needs, he placed a hand on the front door and allowed it to creak open.

The second he entered, it slammed behind him.

But that didn't scare him.

Nor did the lack of door handle or way out. He knew he'd find a way out. He trusted that much.

"April!" he shouted out.

Nothing.

He was standing in one large room, a sea of echoing black. He found a switch on the wall and a light came on, revealing a body crumpled on the floor.

He knew whose body it was straight away.

He edged closer to where April lay. The first time he'd seen her in so long. Her body covered in knife wounds, remnants of the method of murder left stained upon her corpse.

Oscar knelt down beside her and stroked his hand down her soft hair. As he did, he leant down lower, whispered gently in her ear:

"You don't fool me."

He pressed the crucifix hard against the image and it fell straight through. So strange; a moment ago he'd believed it, and he touched it – but now he didn't, its corporeal form was penetrated and it dissolved into fragments of nothing.

He stood, looking around the room.

"I come to You in Christ's name, putting on Your full armour, so that I can take my stand against the devil's schemes."

He lifted his crucifix and pushed it as far as his arm could reach, then rotated, displaying it to the room, forcing it upon the false creation.

"For our struggle is not against flesh and blood, but against the powers of this dark world and the spiritual forces of evil."

The darkness disintegrated.

The room fell away, bit by bit, discarded into the air.

"In this day of evil, I stand my ground."

Upon the front door, the handle presented itself again.

"Standing firm with the belt of truth buckled around my waist, and with my feet readied by the gospel of peace."

Whimpering.

He could hear whimpering.

Whimpering that felt real. Not some trick, or some image,

or hallucination or presentation or whatever it wished to be called – it was a person's. A man's.

"No…" came a desperate voice amongst the begging. "Please…"

In the centre of a living room left to rot, with ageing furniture and a dusty fireplace and windowsill that grew mould – was Julian.

He held something in his arms. Nothing, in fact. But Oscar knew Julian believed he held something. Someone he was crying over.

"Please, April, wake up…"

Oscar knew that this wasn't over.

For him, maybe – but not for Julian.

Oscar walked to Julian's body, the quivering wreck, Julian completely oblivious.

"I ask You to give me the gift of discerning spirits so that I may remove evil beings from this home, and from this person, and from his soul."

Oscar knelt next to Julian. Placed a hand on his back that went unnoticed.

It was a strange sight to see Julian as such a wreck. A man who was so proud, so eager to be in charge – to be driven to the brink of his emotional turmoil and be visibly so, was not something done to Julian easily.

Oscar, however, kept calm. Retained his belief in what he was doing. His faith that Julian would see the truth. That Julian could, like he would, recognise the false images of fear that impressed themselves upon his eyes.

"I ask that Your Holy Spirit dwell here with me and my friend, and that you will lead us and guide us through."

Julian looked surprised. He lifted his hands, as if whatever he saw was falling away, was crumbling through his fingers.

"No, I – what's happening?"

"Send us angelic assistance to help us with the removal of these evil spirits."

Julian turned to Oscar.

"What? What are you doing?"

"You can see me?"

"What?"

"Julian, this isn't real. Just concentrate on that. This isn't real."

Julian looked perplexed. He turned back to the room and surveyed his surroundings, peering up and down the walls, the walls that now formed the room that Oscar saw.

"Finally, send to war those that can fight these demonic powers I cannot handle. Leave Julian in His name, and keep him in Your peace."

"Oscar?" Julian looked around himself again, to his arms, then back to Oscar. "What's happening?"

"Julian, listen to me – this wasn't real. Everything you saw from entering this house was created to trap you in here. To keep you here."

"I – I – I saw April…"

"It wasn't real, Julian. It wasn't real."

Julian covered his face.

Oscar didn't have time for this.

"Look, I know it's hard to take, I know it's a lot, but right now, I need your help – I need to know where April is. Where is she?"

Julian dropped his hands and looked upwards, as if searching for the answer.

"We got separated…"

"That's fine, which way did she go?"

Julian looked to the door, then back to Oscar.

"Please," Oscar persisted. "It is absolutely integral that we find April as soon as we can. Where is she?

"I – I – I don't know."

5 0

THE STALE, SALTY AIR OF EARTH FELT FRESH FOR THE FIRST TIME in centuries.

This time, the devil did answer his call.

"Agramon."

"Yes?"

"You have done well."

"Thank you, my lord."

"We may not have much time."

"I understand."

"We will start immediately."

And from the moment it was decided, almost instantaneously, he could feel Hell flowing through him, he could feel the flames licking his ankles, the fire burning through his arms, his muscles twinging with the excitement of a new dawn – a new dawn that would never end, a new dawn that would never be dawn again, a destructive dawn, collapsing into a permanent state of forever.

How many demons would have previously seeped through Hell's gates just to share the soul of some pathetic human?

With the balance as it was, it would have been ten or so,

maybe – most of which would be thwarted by Heaven's warriors. Those few had little time to incite the evil they did.

But what of those times when possession had exceeded that – when the balance had changed? When it wasn't ten or so, when it was close to a hundred?

In Europe from 1939 through to 1945, in Ukraine from 1932 through to 1933, in Cambodia 1975 to 1979 – the excess spill-over allowed them to give the nudge, to tamper with the balance.

That was close to a hundred.

They celebrated that hundred like it was the best thing that could happen.

Now this was thousands.

And he could feel every one of them. Taking bodies, sharing it with a pure soul – a soul that they would discharge from its skin. Within years the world would be tearing itself apart and Hell would reclaim its rightful place – and it was down to him.

Down to Agramon.

A fear demon.

They'd laughed at him.

No one was laughing at him now.

No one.

The clear, blue sky had been shining for too long. Now, it ended. Sparse white clouds parted for excess grey clumps of rain. A rumble of thunder shook the distance, shook it and didn't stop, accompanied by lightning, flashing all around.

This was not a coincidence.

This was it.

He could feel his skin getting weaker. He could, but there was no fear – he didn't need it for long. Once they were all ready, he'd shed his confines and expose his true image to a world that would go to their knees, pray for mercy, and call him God.

That's how fickle they were.

See something powerful, they'll worship it.

Their real God would be brushed aside for an evil deity who could act out their commands.

"Thank you, Oscar," he whispered to the wind as he held his hands out, lifted his face, closed his eyes and felt the harsh sting of rain droplets pound his face into moisture, stealing his perspiration, stinging nothing, savouring everything.

It was his.

No, it was theirs.

It was all theirs.

OSCAR GUIDED JULIAN OUT OF THE HOUSE, LAYING HIM ON THE front lawn. Oscar had never seen Julian this weak – whatever Julian had seen, whatever he'd been through, had pushed him as far as he could handle.

Which only made Oscar more worried about April.

As soon as Julian was laid comfortably on the floor he ran back in – yes, Julian needed help, needed watching, but even more desperately than that, April needed saving.

"April!" he shouted.

He darted through the front room, through to what looked to have been a kitchen; though it was more of a cesspit for flies and germs. The sink was overflowing with rotten plates, the window was lined with damp, and the true colour of the floor tiles was indecipherable.

"April!" he tried again.

He made a full circle back to the front door, passing stairs on the way. Having had no success on the lower floor, he leapt up the stairs two at a time.

"April?"

Screaming – unmistakable screaming, coming from a nearby open door.

Oscar arrived into the room, presenting his crucifix.

She was pinned to the wall. Her arms out wide, wriggling against her own constraints, closing her eyes and flinching away.

Seeing her again was magical – seeing her like this was heart-wrenching. For so long he'd pictured their reunion, seen her face, wished he'd be next to her once more. Now he was, he had to will himself not to run.

"No, Oscar!" she cried. "Oscar, please, she's not your daughter... She's not your daughter..."

Oscar's knees wobbled and his resolve weakened as he realised what April was seeing.

With a new lease of energy he strode forward, pushing his crucifix out before him.

He'd brought her back before, he'd do it again.

"Father, hear me now," he spoke, determined, his voice strong and emotionless, his focus entirely on her. "I break and loosen myself and my loves from any vows I made, any demons entering through the bloodlines – I cancel all invitations made to unclean spirits."

"No! Oscar, please, no!"

"I renounce the lies, the fear, the hatred and the anger that may have kept me from You, and pray you set me free from my sins."

He pushed the crucifix against her chest, harder, feeling it tinge but pressing nonetheless, must not falter, must not let her down.

"Oscar... don't hurt me..."

He flinched away, closed his eyes for a moment, unable to take what she was seeing; him, in an attempt to hurt her.

Was that what her deepest fear was?

That he would harm her in some way?

"She's not your daughter... Please, Oscar, she's not your daughter..."

That hurt even more. The unbearable knowledge that not only was she seeing Oscar at his rageful worst, but that he was with the creature who had turned him into a homicidal assailant.

Oscar and Hayley back together again.

This only made him push the crucifix harder, say his prayers with more gusto – he could not bear to think that this was what April was seeing.

"I ask for your legion of angels to station themselves around us, to attack every unclean spirit, to remove all false deities from the mind of this servant of Yours."

April convulsed, as if she was being stabbed, gutted, and she choked. Blood spilled from her mouth, and this was proving more difficult than Oscar had anticipated; she believed in these images so much that they were beginning to harm her.

"I bind the principalities, powers, rulers of darkness, spiritual wickedness, not to transfer but to be disbanded and sent back to Hell."

April screamed harder, a wound on the side of her neck appearing, expanding wider into a lengthening circle, trickling red.

"Demons, I command you to manifest and remove yourself, in His name I command you to the pit!"

"Oscar..."

"I send the Holy Spirit to burn you, to truth, in His name, I command you, leave this place!"

April spluttered another mouthful.

"Come on, April."

"It's not going to work, you know," came the cocky voice of a child behind him.

A glance over his soldier showed Hayley standing there, body of a child, face of malice.

"You're not real," Oscar said, unsure whether it was directed at Hayley, or to himself.

"I'm always real," Hayley replied. "And she's going to die, and you're going to have to watch."

THEN

5 2

THIS WAS THE LAST PLACE OSCAR THOUGHT HE'D BE, BUT somehow it was where he ended up. After all, he'd said his peace to April, and his train wasn't for a while.

Still, he felt he owed this much to Julian.

"And where do you think you're going to start?" Julian asked, sitting on his garden bench with a coffee, Oscar sipping his water, having denied Julian's offer of a beverage.

"God, I don't know. I guess Italy would be somewhere to start. Or, there's stuff in Derek's journals about The Skulls of Cambodia, that there's still evil lingering there to access. There's also some people mentioned."

"So you're going, and you don't even know where you're going to?"

"I'll figure it out once I get to the airport."

Julian sipped his coffee then watched Oscar, waiting a beat, his expression the same judgemental blankness Oscar was so used to.

"You know you're making a stupid decision, right?"

"Julian, don't."

"Don't come here if you don't want the truth. I'm going to give it to you."

"I'm not making a stupid decision."

"You're right. You're making an awful decision. The worst decision you've ever made."

Oscar sighed. Considered leaving, in fact, readied himself to get up, but Julian drew him back in.

"You messed up. You couldn't help it. Get over it."

Oscar scoffed – it was that simple, was it?

"I tried to kill her."

"Yes, whilst under control of a–"

"I can't do this again."

"Do what again?"

"This same conversation. You think I haven't had it with myself a million times?"

"Oh yeah? And when you have it with yourself, what does yourself say back?"

Oscar stood. Enough.

"What, so if you don't like the truth, you bail?"

"I'm not bailing."

"Yes, you are, you're getting up to go."

"I don't know why I came here."

"For honesty?"

"No, I guess I thought I owed you something. You defended April against me, and I appreciated that."

"I didn't do it as a favour to you, Oscar, I did it because it's April, and I have known and cared for her for longer than you have."

"Oh, well you win then."

Oscar turned and began to march to the garden gate. He halted when Julian stood and addressed him with vigour in his voice Oscar was reluctant to hear.

"You go now, don't think about re-entering her life. Not at least without a damn good epiphany."

"You may not get this, Julian – but you are not my boss, nor are you hers. We can do what we want with our relationship, and it will be nothing to do with you."

"Oscar, don't you get it? This is bigger than us."

Oscar threw his hands in the air.

"Bigger than what?"

"This fight, it's bigger than the little squabbles you have in your relationship."

"You think this is a squabble?"

"It's not significant."

"I tried to kill her!"

"And you failed! Because we beat it, and she's still alive, she still wants you, because she knows it's not as black-and-white as you're making it out to be!"

"Not making it out to be black-and-white."

"Then don't be so stupid as to get on that train."

The argument ceased for a fleeting moment of reflection.

Discarded words that had poured out of their mouths dissolved between them, leaving nothing but a bad taste on the air.

"Let me just ask you one question," Julian proposed. "Then you can go. And I won't stop you."

"You can't stop me."

"Right, yes – but let me just ask you this question."

"Fine."

Julian paused, ready to articulate himself as best as he could.

"Imagine you had a decision. The fate of the world or the fate of April. Which would you choose?"

"That's a ridiculous hypothetical situation."

"Not really. Your battle was against the demon parading itself as your daughter, not with April. But you've taken a battle about Heaven and Hell and made it about your relationship, which it isn't, and that is where your fault lies – because to you,

April comes first, and your responsibility comes second. It just can't be that way."

"You don't know a thing about me."

"Then tell me I'm wrong."

Oscar opened the garden fence and loitered.

"Which would you choose?" Oscar decided to ask.

"The fate of the world. Every time."

"Wow. You answered so quickly it was as if April's fate wasn't even a consideration."

"It can't be, Oscar. Neither can mine. Neither can yours. This is bigger than us, and that is what you are not realising by doing this."

"No, Julian. It's you who isn't realising."

"Realising what?"

Oscar hesitated.

"That it shouldn't even be a question."

He left, not willing to engage in any more of the pointless debate.

He left, with Julian's question playing on his mind, wondering whether he would have the impetus to do what he must, should it come down to it.

And he realised – he wasn't doing any of this for the sake of the world.

Even at the beginning, the deeper realisation of what was at stake never fought in his mind. He wasn't fighting for the world.

He was always doing it for her.

NOW

53

THE SIGHT OF THAT CHILD WAS ALMOST ENOUGH TO SEND OSCAR back into his own spiral of madness.

"I'm not even the one killing her," Hayley stated, her voice cheerful and bouncy. "It's you."

"It's not me."

Why was he responding to it? He scolded himself, reminding him that you never pander to the taunts of a demon or evil spirit; that was a beginner's lesson, and he should know better.

He turned back to April.

"April, come on, it's me."

She cried and wept and whimpered and struggled some more.

Her throat was bleeding now. This was just a small wound, but how long until it was bigger?

"Almighty, we beg you to keep the evil spirit from further molesting this servant of Yours."

"He's not listening."

He pressed the crucifix hard, hard against her chest, hard against her heart, pushing it into her, further into her.

"May the goodness and peace of our redeemer take possession of this woman."

Please, April. Please.

"May we no longer fear any evil since You are with us, who lives and reigns in Your unity."

"Oscar…" She spoke so softly, it was as if she was saying it to the voices inside her head.

"It's useless," Hayley taunted.

Oscar ignored it.

"You're pathetic."

"And those who have done good shall enter into everlasting life, as those who have done good shall be freed."

"Oscar?" April lifted her eyes to his, and they met.

"Why are you doing this?" she asked, so innocently, so gentle.

"I'm not, April, it's not me – and you have to fight it."

"You hurt me…"

"No, April, I didn't – I would never hurt you. Change my divinity into flesh, He is one, not by mixture of substance, but by oneness of His person."

"Oscar… what's going on…"

Her head drooped, as if she was falling back in, but Oscar dropped his crucifix so he could put both hands on the side of her face, hold her feet, keep his eyes on hers.

"Keep looking into my eyes, April, keep looking."

"You can't save her…"

"Keep looking – this is me, April. This is the real me. I'm back, and I'm never going to hurt you – *I* am real, *I* am here."

"Oscar…"

She reached out a hand and rested it on his face.

She could move. Her arms could move. She was coming back, he was almost there, he knew it, he could feel it.

"To deal in mercy with our Father and be mindful of His only covenant."

April fell from her position against the wall into a feeble mess on the floor. She struggled to her knees, her eyes widening and narrowing, flashing between what was real and what was not.

Oscar could see the struggle, but he was so close, so close.

"Be enlightened and shine forth, and begone this evil spirit from Your servant, begone."

"You won't–"

Oscar lifted his crucifix once more and threw his arm out toward the childish wretch who once placed its full control over him, who thought it could taunt him, stop him from saving April – the pathetic little bitch who had no idea who she was dealing with.

"Turn back the evil on my foes and in your faithfulness destroy them – begone spirit!" he screamed at it. "I compel you from this place! I compel you from this person!"

Hayley's face morphed into a helpless morsel that had nowhere to go and nothing to help her.

"Begone – from all distress you rescued me, now rescue me once more, and clean this unclean spirit!"

Hayley's image distorted. April watched with confused realisation.

"Look down upon my enemies and begone – cast this out from here and let us be free."

The child dissolved into matter and trickled into wherever it was aggressive spirits went.

Oscar turned back to April and went to put his arms around her – but she scuttled away, pushing herself against the wall.

"April, that wasn't me," Oscar insisted. "It wasn't. It was an image created by a demon. This is me, this is the real me."

She looked him up and down, torn between confusion and relief.

"April, really. I'm back. It's gone, and it's okay."

Another hesitation on her part, then she flung herself into Oscar's arms. He held her tightly, and she squeezed back just as hard.

Her smell, her touch, her warm embrace – it was better than he'd imagined.

They were reunited.

And now they were going to have to face the world that the saving of her soul had created together.

54

Little Andy, a seven-year-old choir boy from Berkshire, disrupted his parents' garden party in order to stab his fork into the throat of their elderly neighbour with such gusto that it tore her gullet in two.

Lucy from Chicago, an eleven-year-old prodigy in the ballet world, interrupted her lesson in order to tell her ballet instructor to keep his "incessantly searching tongue" from her "ugly pre-pubescent cunt."

On the streets of Rome, a number of pre-schoolers escaped their nursey by pouring boiled water from kettles hidden away in the office over the unfortunate adults minding them so they could descend on the Vatican with offensive slurs.

A promising young doctor named Kungawo made the headlines in South Africa when he stood in the midst of an exam, walked slowly to the front of the hall, and ripped the exam invigilator's hair from their body. As shock hung over the rest of the students studying for their opportunity to become a surgeon, he then pulled out her teeth and skull-fucked her with a screwdriver that he was unable to remember how he'd attained.

All over the world, chaos ensued – the most prominent countries for third-world, middle-class corruption proving to be the easiest targets.

Children were most affected, though young adults and middle-aged sinners carried out attacks also. There was one case of a woman suffering from Alzheimer's who sodomised their carer with a broken wine bottle. The carer, a twenty-three-year-old man, was unable to explain how the pensioner had managed to have enough strength to pin him down and assault him.

Governments were calling for emergency meetings, though not one could articulate what for. They were aware there was some kind of crisis, but what? People were acting crazier? Mental health had a sudden boom?

How were they supposed to produce a manifesto that could solve that?

A team was put together to try to answer these questions, but after constant studying and scrutiny, they finally confessed to the public what the public had already suspected – every test they did was inconclusive, and every hypothesis proven ridiculous.

The Church knew, of course. And their silent treatment toward the Sensitives only revealed part of the resentment they felt. This silent treatment couldn't last, of course, as when you wage a war, you need your best warriors on your side – and the Sensitives were the only ones who gave them a fighting chance.

Although, to refer to it as a fighting chance would be to underestimate the damage that had been caused. It was better termed as denial or over-optimistic hope. The Church was prepared to go down fighting, but they could all see it in each other's eyes – this was the end.

Agramon sat back and watched. He was made prince of Hell and would be made prince of Earth once their invasion was complete. Once bodies were snatched and terrible acts committed, enough evil would be formed for them to surface in their true form.

Meanwhile, little Stacey was fed up of being bullied, and when the orthodontist went to put her braces in, she bit off his finger and swallowed it whole. She laughed and wiped blood on his white coat as she removed his front teeth with a plier.

In the end, the newspaper reports had to be censored.

Though in truth, they didn't even know what to report anymore.

One thing was certain.

Someone, somewhere, had caused something that would be unlikely to ever be undone.

FOUR DAYS LATER

55

JULIAN DIDN'T SPEAK TO OSCAR; HE BARELY EVEN acknowledged him. Oscar felt like he should be grateful for not having to enter dialogue that always felt like he was being criticised, but the silence only confirmed that Oscar had done something that many would deem as unforgivable.

April spoke to him, of course. He'd returned to their home and changed into clean clothes that he'd left. She was grateful for being saved, but even in her eyes, he could still see it; he was being judged.

One day, he decided to broach the subject.

"You're disappointed in me, aren't you?" he asked.

April hesitated. Looked at the dinner she'd been prodding with her fork for ten minutes. As if she knew this question was coming, but she wasn't quite ready for the answer.

"Well, how can I be?" she asked. "You saved my life. I can't be ungrateful for that."

"Be honest with me, April."

"I am being honest."

"You think I made the wrong decision, don't you?"

April looked to him, a face full of denied pain, devastatingly blank, deprived of all irrationality and rationality until nothing was left.

"What do you want me to say?" was her answer, and Oscar left it at that. They finished tea in silence and, when April went upstairs following an announcement she was having a bath, Oscar took his beer and walked into the garden.

There had been no sunshine for a while. It seemed as if summer had come to a very sudden halt, like one minute it was there, the next it was gone. Vague raindrops landed on him, but he didn't mind. His hoodie kept him warm, and he liked the rain; he'd always been grateful for it.

A car alarm started somewhere in the distance.

A scream and a smash sounded from one of their neighbours.

A tremble in the ground rumbled, following something shaking.

Oscar went back inside. All of this was because of him and, however unproductive it was, it was best to conceal himself from it. To hide away from its truth.

It seemed no matter what he did, he always created a bad situation for people.

What he'd give to just go back to that moment when April announced she was pregnant. To know then what series of events it was going to lead to.

Or, what if he'd never left? What if he'd listened to Julian in the garden – however dreadful a thought listening to Julian was.

The sad acknowledgement that Julian had turned out to be right occurred more times than Oscar was willing to admit.

He slowly trudged up the stairs and found himself at the bathroom door, the blockade between him and April.

He knocked gently.

"April, can I come in?"

He wasn't sure why he was there, what he was going to say,

or even why his feet had brought him to her. Somehow, that was where he ended up.

"Yes."

He entered. Her body was disguised by bubbles, but the skin above her breasts was still enough to tease him into excitement at the sight of her; then he realised he should be feeling bad, and his excitement caused him a tinge of guilt.

He knelt beside the bath and took her hand in his.

"I'm sorry," Oscar said. "I'm sorry that I saved you."

"Oscar, don't–"

"But, in all honesty, I'd do it again."

She looked back at him, slightly stunned.

"A little while ago, Julian said that if it came down to the world or you, I would have to be prepared to make the right choice. But, to me, I did. And I would save you every time."

He placed his hand on her hair, brushed his fingers down-wards, and her eyes returned, that same lost expression she had whenever she was caught up in her love for him.

"I'm sorry if that has messed things up for everyone."

"Look, Oscar, I'm grateful to be alive – but look at what it's cost everyone. If this was what being alive was going to feel like, then I'd have been better off dead."

Oscar forced a false smile.

"We've handled bad before."

"Yes, but never bad like this."

"Well, okay, Derek has. He handled it before."

"Where is Derek now?"

He sighed, looked down, then thought.

"Maybe we should just give in," April said. "Maybe we should just admit that, this time, we've done everything we can, and it wasn't enough. Try and enjoy our last days before every-thing ends."

Oscar shook his head. "But we haven't, have we?"

"What?"

"Done everything we can."

"Oscar–"

"I don't think we should give in so easily."

"We'll lose."

"That's what we always say."

April laughed a reluctant laugh.

"I'll go with whatever you say," Oscar told her. "Because whatever side I'm on, I want it to be yours."

"You can't put a decision like that on me."

"Yes I can. Because I'm not fighting for the world. I'm fighting for you. Always you."

Her hand reached out and found Oscar's, their fingers interlocking as her face spelled out a million emotions, each one of them relating to love.

"So," Oscar said. "What's it going to be?"

And in her smile, he found his answer.

JOIN RICK WOOD'S READER'S GROUP AND GET TWO BOOKS FOR FREE

Join at www.rickwoodwriter.com/sign-up

THE SENSITIVES BOOK SIX: REPENT
AVAILABLE NOW

RICK
WOOD

REPENT

THE
SENSITIVES
BOOK
SIX

ALSO BY RICK WOOD

The Sensitives:

Book One – The Sensitives

Book Two – My Exorcism Killed Me

Book Three – Close to Death

Book Four – Demon's Daughter

Book Five – Questions for the Devil

Book Six - Repent

Book Seven - The Resurgence

Book Eight - Until the End

Shutter House

Shutter House

Prequel Book One - This Book is Full of Bodies

Cia Rose:

Book One – After the Devil Has Won

Book Two – After the End Has Begun

Book Three - After the Living Have Lost

Chronicles of the Infected

Book One – Zombie Attack

Book Two – Zombie Defence

Book Three – Zombie World

Standalones:

When Liberty Dies

I Do Not Belong

Death of the Honeymoon

Sean Mallon:

Book One – The Art of Murder

Book Two – Redemption of the Hopeless

The Edward King Series:

Book One – I Have the Sight

Book Two – Descendant of Hell

Book Three – An Exorcist Possessed

Book Four – Blood of Hope

Book Five – The World Ends Tonight

Non-Fiction

How to Write an Awesome Novel

Thrillers published as Ed Grace:

The Jay Sullivan Thriller Series

Assassin Down

Kill Them Quickly

Printed in the USA
CPSIA information can be obtained
at www.ICGtesting.com
LVHW042202311024
795404LV00033B/355

9 781838 084349